THE BOBBSEY TWINS
IN MEXICO

THE BOBBSEY TWINS BOOKS
By Laura Lee Hope

As Bert and Freddie drew near, they saw that the animal
in the cage was a bobcat.

The Bobbsey Twins
in Mexico

By

LAURA LEE HOPE

GROSSET & DUNLAP
Publishers   *New York*

CONTENTS

THE BOBBSEY TWINS
IN MEXICO

CHAPTER I

EXCITING NEWS

THE Bobbsey twins were entertaining a caller in the living room of their home.

"Are you going to be away a long time, Mrs. Martin?" Flossie Bobbsey asked politely.

Mrs. Martin, who lived directly across the street, smiled at the little blonde girl.

"Yes," she replied. "My husband and I will be away two or three months. I hope you will take good care of the family that is coming to live in our house."

Flossie's twin brother Freddie, who looked very much like her, sat near them. He said, "Sure we will. I'll show the children all my fire engines and they can play with some of them, too."

Freddie Bobbsey was proud of his collection of fire engines. He had one so small that he could hold it on his little finger. The largest was so big that he could hardly pull it on the sidewalk, and it had a hose which squirted real water.

1

"I'm sure the children from Mexico will want to see your fire engines, Freddie," said Mrs. Martin, "and your dolls too, Flossie."

"Oh!" cried Flossie. "I'd better get my dolls cleaned up. They need to be washed and ironed. Will you please 'scuse me, Mrs. Martin?"

Mrs. Martin nodded. The boy and girl sitting across the room began to laugh. They were Nan and Bert Bobbsey, who were also twins but a few years older than Freddie and Flossie.

"If you wash and iron your dolls, there won't be much left of them, Flossie," laughed Nan.

Flossie hardly paid attention. She was already skipping out of the room on her way to get her dolls' clothes. Nan and Bert asked Mrs. Martin to tell them more about the Mexican family that was going to move into her house. When they learned that Mr. Castillio, the father, was in the chocolate business, and was coming to Lakeport to see about opening a candy factory, the twins' eyes opened wide in delight.

"Mrs. Castillio is coming too, and I believe they are bringing a Mexican Indian woman who has looked after the children since they were born."

Mrs. Martin said that the boy was Bert's and Nan's age, and that the little girl was the same age as Freddie and Flossie.

"Can they speak English?" Nan asked.

"Oh, yes, indeed," Mrs. Martin replied. "They can speak English better than I can speak Spanish."

As Bert and Nan knew, nearly everyone in Mexico speaks Spanish. Only a few of the Indians who live far away from the cities have languages of their own.

"I can't speak any Spanish," said Bert. "Maybe I ought to learn some before the Castillios move in."

Mrs. Martin laughed. She remarked that one could not learn to speak Spanish in a few hours, and that the new family would be in Lakeport in two days.

"Then I guess we'll all have to speak English," said Bert. "Mrs. Martin, I've heard that people in Mexico don't eat the same things we do. If we should invite the children to dinner sometime we wouldn't know what to give them."

Mrs. Martin said it was true that the Mexican ways of preparing food were somewhat different from those in the United States, but that the food these dishes were made of did not differ from the kind of food the Bobbsey children ate.

"But maybe sometime they will invite you to their house to dinner and then you can see how you like tamales and other Mexican dishes," Mrs. Martin told them.

She rose to go and the twins stood up too, and walked to the front door with her.

For the next two days Freddie and Flossie spent

most of their daytime hours watching the house across the street. They saw the expressman come and take away two trunks for the Martins. A few hours later a taxicab drew up and waited at the curb. Mr. and Mrs. Martin, carrying four suitcases and a dog basket, came out of the house.

"Oh, they're going to take their dog Flippy with them!" exclaimed Flossie. "I wish I was that dog right now!"

Freddie giggled. "You mean you'd like to be shut up in the basket with the lid down over your head?" he asked.

"Oh, Freddie, you know I don't mean that," said Flossie. "But I love to go on trips and I don't think dogs do. Maybe Mrs. Martin should have left Flippy here and taken me with her."

Freddie reminded his twin that if she were to go away she could not meet the Mexican children who were coming to live in the Martin house. Flossie admitted this, and said she guessed they would have more fun staying home after all.

At bedtime the following day, Mrs. Bobbsey had hard work getting her smaller children upstairs. They were afraid the Castillios might move in during the night and they would miss seeing them. The twins were envious of their older brother and sister, who could stay up two hours longer. On the way upstairs Flossie whispered to Freddie:

"Let's stay awake and when Nan and Bert come to bed we'll ask them what happened."

Flossie slept in a room with Nan, and Freddie shared one with Bert. Freddie thought Flossie's idea was good, but alas! the twins could not carry out the little scheme. One minute after their heads touched the pillows they were sound asleep.

But they need not have worried. The Castillios did not move in during the night nor did they come the next day, nor the next. The four Bobbsey twins began to grow concerned.

"Oh, Nan," Flossie said to her sister as they were dressing on the morning of the fourth day since the Martins had left, "what do you suppose has happened to the chocolate man and his family?"

Nan shrugged. "Maybe they're coming in a car," she said, "and it broke down."

"Maybe they're coming in a plane and it got lost in the clouds," suggested Flossie.

At that moment thunderous yells came from the hall, and the sounds of someone clumping.

Nan and Flossie, wondering what was happening, rushed to the door. When they looked out, they saw Freddie stomping up and down the hall, clapping his hand back and forth against his mouth and whooping loudly. He had on an Indian suit with a tall feather hat which he had worn on Hallowe'en. The girls laughed.

"Are you a Mexican Indian?" Nan asked him.

"No speak English," Freddie replied, and continued his mad dance up and down the hall.

Now Freddie became a little too excited playing Indian. Not content with clumping forward, he suddenly decided to clump backward. Before anyone could warn him he reached the top of the stairway, lost his balance, and fell.

"Oh!" screamed Flossie as she saw arms, legs, and feathers sliding down the steps.

Freddie might have gone all the way to the landing and received a very hard bump if Dinah, the Negro cook, had not been on her way up the stairs. As she reached the landing she saw Freddie tumbling toward her. A moment later she had swooped him up in her arms.

"Mah goodness, chile!" she exclaimed. "Ef yo' is gwine be an Indian yo' bettah live in a tent wif no stairs in it."

Freddie was not hurt, though he had been mighty scared for a few seconds. But when Dinah spoke about a tent with no stairs in it, he not only forgot to be scared but began to laugh. Imagine a tent *with* stairs in it!

"Yo' breakfast am ready," Dinah announced. "Yo' all bettah come and eat it so yo' all will be through before those new people move in."

"You mean you know when they're coming?" cried Nan excitedly.

Dinah said that her husband Sam, who also lived at the Bobbsey house, and sometimes drove the car, had been downtown early to the meat market. The butcher had told him that he had received a tele-phone call from Mr. Castillio, ordering meat to be delivered that very morning.

Mr. Bobbsey had already left for his lumber com-pany office when all four twins finally assembled at the breakfast table, but Mrs. Bobbsey was there. Freddie and Flossie could hardly wait to go outside and watch for the arrival of the Castillio family. But their mother insisted that they finish breakfast first, and she cautioned the children not to bother the new neighbors.

"Give them time to unpack and get settled," she directed. "You'll have plenty of time to become ac-quainted."

As the Bobbsey twins went outside they had every intention of obeying their mother's instructions. But when a taxicab drew up to the Martin home and two persons alighted from it, Freddie forgot all about what his mother had said. He dashed across the street to watch as bag after bag was taken from the cab. A moment later Flossie joined him. Though Nan called to them to come back across the street, they paid no attention.

"Flossie, there aren't any children," whispered Freddie to his sister.

This was indeed true. Only a man and a woman

had got out of the cab and were climbing the porch steps of the house.

Flossie, disappointed not to see any children, hurried up the steps and, looking up at the newcomers, said in a sad voice:

"I thought you were going to bring your children. I've been waiting for four days to play with your little girl."

CHAPTER II

THE MEXICAN DOG

THE man and woman on the porch looked down at Flossie Bobbsey. She had appeared so suddenly that it almost seemed as if a fairy had landed on the porch right out of the air.

"*Duende!*" exclaimed the woman.

Flossie just stared. She did not know what the word meant. But how could she? Duende was a Spanish word meaning an elf. To be polite, she said:

"My name is Flossie Bobbsey. I live across the street. Mrs. Martin asked me and my brothers and sister to play with your children, but you didn't bring your children. I'm very sorry, Mr. Castillio."

This was a long speech for Flossie, but the man and woman did not interrupt her. At the end of it they smiled.

"I am not Señor Castillio," said the man. "He will come in a little while with Mateo and Marina."

By this time Freddie, Nan, and Bert had joined their little sister.

9

"Are Mateo and Marina the names of the children?" Bert asked.

The man nodded his head and said that Mateo was a boy about Bert's age, and that Marina was six years old. The man explained further that he and his wife Anita had come on ahead to get the house ready for the Castillios and to cook dinner. The family would arrive about noon.

"Then I can play with—" Flossie started to say.

She stopped short when she saw the head of a tiny animal pop out of the front of the man's buttoned coat. The children had never seen an animal like it.

The Bobbsey twins, of course, were used to surprises. Ever since they could remember, their father and mother, and even Dinah and Sam, had planned all sorts of interesting surprises for them. They had been on several trips, and had had many wonderful adventures.

During the previous winter, for instance, an exciting thing had happened. Mr. Bobbsey had received a letter mailed thirty years before. Through this the twins had solved a mystery, and had enjoyed a grand vacation at Sugar Maple Hill.

But in all the places they had visited, they had never seen a little animal like the one that was pulling itself up from under the man's coat. It had a tiny head and ears, and big, bright eyes.

"Is it a tiny, tiny deer?" Flossie asked.

The Mexican woman explained that the tiny animal was not a deer but a little dog. At her suggestion they all went into the house, for the little dog was shivering with cold. Freddie was thinking that if their big old dog, Snap, should open his mouth very wide, he could almost put the little Mexican dog inside it!

"Pedro," Anita said to her husband, "put Chito on the sofa so the children can see him."

Pedro set down the wee dog, which was only seven inches long. Unlike most dogs, he had no hair on him. Bert and Nan remembered now having heard about the Mexican hairless dog, named Chihuahua.

Chito was very friendly, and did not run away from the twins. He let each one of them hold him, but he seemed to take a special liking to Nan. Pedro said this was because Chito liked to snuggle into her jacket as she held him.

Flossie explained about their own dogs, Snap and Waggo. Snap was old and would not hurt anybody, but Waggo was a young fox terrier, and very playful. Waggo never meant to hurt anything, but sometimes he played too hard, and then dogs, or furniture, or even people got hurt.

"I'll explain to Waggo all about Chito," Flossie said. "And then Waggo can introduce him to other dogs in Lakeport."

Pedro and his wife laughed. They told Flossie she

was very kind, but that Chito was not used to playing with other dogs and was content to stay in the
house.

Nan knew Pedro and Anita had work to do, so she
suggested the twins go home. They would come back
after the Castillio children and their parents arrived.

As they reached the sidewalk, Bert saw one of his
father's lumber trucks coming up the street. Sam,
who was at the wheel, stopped in front of the Bobbsey house.

"Where are you going, Sam?" Freddie cried out.
"Please, may I have a ride?"

"Well, I don't rightly know," Sam replied. "S'pose
yo' ask yo' mother." His face broke into a broad
grin, showing his snow-white teeth. "But I 'spect
Mrs. Bobbsey will say yes."

As a matter of fact, Mr. Bobbsey had suggested to
Sam that he stop at the house to see if the boys would
like to go along.

Freddie ran into the house and a moment later
dashed out, saying his mother had given permission
for Bert and him to ride along with Sam. They
hopped up on the seat beside him, and he started the
motor. Two blocks away they stopped at a red light.

On the sidewalk stood a boy a little older and a
little bigger than Bert. He was Danny Rugg, a mean
boy who liked to pick fights. Both Bert and Freddie

had had several tussles with him, and each time they hoped it would be the last.

"Where you going?" Danny called out.

"I don't know," Bert replied.

"You do so," said Danny, "and I want to go with you."

Bert and Freddie did not want him along, and, as a matter of fact, Sam did not either. The light changed and Sam started the truck. But Danny was determined not to be left behind. Racing from the curbstone, he made a flying leap and caught hold of a couple of boards which stuck out from the back of the truck. A second later there was a scream from someone on the sidewalk, and a cry from behind the truck. Danny Rugg had fallen from his perch!

There were cars coming from both directions. Fortunately, the woman's scream had warned motorists in time to pull their cars out of the way.

Danny was unhurt except for a bump on his head, but he was very angry. Sam had pulled up to the curb at the other side of the intersection and now he, Bert, and Freddie ran back to where Danny stood at the corner. There was a crowd around him and he was saying:

"They threw me off the truck!"

"We did nothing of the kind," Bert spoke up hotly. "You had no right to try to climb onto the truck!"

Danny saw a chance to make trouble, and this pleased him. He said that his father would fix the Bobbseys! This made Bert so angry that he was going to fight Danny, but Sam caught his arm. He warned Bert not to touch Danny, saying that the Bobbseys had done nothing wrong, but that if Bert should start a fight, then Danny might have cause for complaint. Sam made sure that Danny was all right, then he told the Bobbsey boys they would go along.

The three of them got back on the truck and drove off. Sam drove a little faster, explaining that he already was late to meet the man at the amusement park.

"Amusement park?" Bert asked. "What amusement park?" He thought he knew all the parks in Lakeport, and none of them had amusements.

Sam grinned. "It's gwine to be an amusement park," he said. "Did yo' evah hear of a travelin' amusement park?"

Bert and Freddie shook their heads.

"Well," said Sam, "it ain't a circus and it ain't a fair and it ain't a carnival."

"Well, then, for goodness sake, what is it?" asked Bert.

Sam found it hard to explain. The man who owned the amusements traveled with all his equipment and his actors and actresses in a small steamer. They traveled from place to place. Before their arrival, certain of his men would come on ahead to get the grounds ready for their show. They had come to Mr. Bobbsey to buy lumber for building more bleachers like the ones they carried with them. People would sit on them to watch certain performances.

"When's the boat coming?" Freddie cried excitedly.

"In a few days," Sam replied.

Freddie determined that he would be down at the dock when the boat came in. He had been too young the last time he had gone to an amusement park to take a ride on the Ferris wheel or knock down the toy rabbits with bean bags, or try for the lucky number and win a box of candy. But now he was big enough to do all these things.

Bert, too, was enthusiastic about the amusement park, for he wanted to shoot at the clay pigeons and enter one of the pony races.

"What do the actors and actresses do?" he asked Sam.

The white-haired Negro shook his head. He did not know, he said, but he thought that they gave a play right on the boat. He told the boys that when he was a young man and lived in the South showboats came up the river twice a year. They had a regular theater on board, and lots of people used to go to the performances.

"Sometimes dey had a special afternoon show fo'

de children," he said. "Maybe dis showboat dat's comin' to Lakeport will have a show fo' yo' all."

Bert and Freddie hoped Sam was right. They had been to plays in the school auditorium, but they had never been to a play on a boat.

Soon Sam turned the truck onto the river road and drove a short distance out of town. Then he turned off the road into a vacant lot, and stopped. This was where he was to leave the lumber.

Bert and Freddie climbed down and ran off a little distance. They knew what Sam was going to do and that they might get hurt if they stood too close to the truck. As soon as they were far enough away, Sam cried out:

"Here I goes, boys!"

CHAPTER III

THE CHOCOLATE MAN'S FAMILY

BOOM! Crack!

With a mighty bang the boards slid from the lumber truck and landed in a neat pile on the ground.

"Oh, he did it. Sam did it!" cried Freddie, jumping up and down. Then he turned a little somersault in his delight.

Yes, Sam had done it again. He knew exactly how to race the lumber truck backward for several feet, then jam on the brake, making the pile of boards slide over the rollers on the truck and land on the ground. But this was not easy to do. Every once in a while one of Mr. Bobbsey's drivers would not stop at just the right second. Then the lumber would slide off only part way and the front of the truck would rise up in the air, its wheels off the ground.

But Sam was an expert. Bert and Freddie never tired of watching him slide the lumber off this way.

"All aboard!" cried Sam. "I'se got to be gettin' back now."

The boys hopped up on the seat beside him and they drove back to the lumberyard. From there the boys would walk home. But first Bert went into his father's office to tell him about Danny Rugg.

"We didn't throw him off, Dad," he said. "We didn't even ask him to ride. Sam didn't know he was climbing up."

"Danny's old enough to know what a dangerous thing that is to do," said Mr. Bobbsey. "I'm sure we'll hear no more about it. Danny knows he was a bad boy and probably will not tell his parents."

But Mr. Bobbsey was wrong, for at that moment the telephone rang. It was Mrs. Rugg calling. Before Mr. Bobbsey could say a word she told him that one of his drivers had been responsible for serious injuries to her son Danny.

"Why, I understood the boy was not hurt," the twins' father told her.

"Indeed he was," Mrs. Rugg cried out. "I shall expect you to do something about it!"

"I'll send a doctor to your house at once," said Mr. Bobbsey. His mouth was very firm as he put down the receiver.

He told Bert and Freddie what Mrs. Rugg had said. The boys could hardly believe what they heard.

"But—but, Dad," said Bert, "we left Danny on the corner and he was all right then."

His father explained that sometimes when a person has a bad fall he does not know until later that he has been seriously injured. It was possible that Danny had been badly hurt after all.

"But—but Sam couldn't help it," Bert insisted.

"No doubt," his father agreed. "Especially since Sam did not know Danny was hanging on behind. But sometimes people can make a lot of trouble for those who are not responsible for accidents."

"You mean you might have to pay a lot of money to Danny if he did get hurt?" Bert wanted to know.

"That's exactly it," Mr. Bobbsey answered, looking very serious.

As Bert and Freddie walked home they were very solemn. But when the two boys reached the street on which they lived, they suddenly forgot to worry about Danny Rugg. In front of their house was a group of people and two cars.

"Looks as if there's been an accident!" cried Bert, starting to run.

Freddie was close on his heels but could not keep up with his brother's longer stride. As Bert reached the group he heard a man say:

"Everything's all right."

Everything did seem to be all right. But on the sidewalk stood Pedro waving his arms about and speaking half in Spanish and half in English. Bert finally got the story.

The little dog Chito had run out of the house.

Waggo, the Bobbseys' fox terrier, had frisked up to him invitingly, but Chito had not understood that Waggo only wanted to play. Frightened, the tiny dog had run into the street.

A motorist coming along had swerved his car to avoid hitting the little dog. In doing this he had got in the path of another car. The driver of that car had had to stop so quickly that a basket of food on the back seat had been thrown against the door. The door had opened and all the food had scattered on the pavement. The last of the food was being picked up and now people were getting back into their cars.

Pedro had Chito down inside his coat. Nan was holding Waggo and scolding him roundly. But Waggo did not understand why he was being scolded. He had only tried to make his new neighbor feel at home.

As Bert came up to Nan, she said worriedly, "We —we'll never be able to play with Mateo and Marina."

"Why not?" Bert asked.

"Because they won't like Waggo. Pedro will tell them what happened. He's very mad," Nan answered.

Bert sighed. It seemed as if all kinds of trouble were coming to the Bobbseys at once. But maybe he could straighten out this difficulty, at least. Going over to Pedro, he said:

"I'm terribly sorry for what happened. Our dog loves to play——"

"And he can do lots of tricks," Freddie interrupted pleadingly. "Want to see some?" As he spoke, Freddie made a sign to Waggo who promptly gave two sharp barks. "Play dead," Freddie commanded, and Waggo immediately went limp in Nan's arms.

At first Pedro did not seem interested in Waggo's tricks, but the little fox terrier was so appealing that he soon forgave him. Nan held Waggo a little nearer Chito and in a few moments he was licking the tiny dog's face. Now they were friends!

The excitement had hardly died down when a taxicab came up the street. It stopped in front of the Martin house.

"They're here!" shouted Freddie.

"Sh——h!" warned Nan. She did not think it very polite for Freddie to greet their new neighbors in such fashion.

From the taxi stepped a very handsome man and a good-looking boy who was just Bert's height. Behind him was the prettiest little girl Nan and Flossie thought they had ever seen. She had long dark curls and large brown eyes. The last person to step from the cab was Mrs. Castillio. She, too, was very pretty. Her daughter Marina looked very much like her, while Mateo looked like his father.

Nan knew that the Bobbseys should not be staring

at the newcomers. At first she thought they should
go back across the street to their own home. But this
did not seem very polite either. Finally she smiled at
the little girl. Marina smiled back. Then Nan stepped
up to Mrs. Castillio.

"We live over there," she said, nodding her head.
"Our name is Bobbsey. We know Mrs. Martin very
well, and—"

She was interrupted by Flossie. "We're glad you're
going to live here," said the small twin, "because
Mrs. Martin hasn't any children for us to play with.
We would like to come over to play with you after
you get your clothes unpacked."

The four Castillios smiled broadly. "We shall be
very glad to see you," said Mrs. Castillio. "I hope
Pedro and Anita have a good dinner waiting for us
because we are very hungry. But after dinner we
shall be happy if you will visit us."

As the Bobbsey children crossed the street, Flossie
said she hoped that Pedro would not tell Mr. and
Mrs. Castillio that Waggo had frightened their dog.
She repeated this to her father when he came home
to luncheon.

"Well, my fat fairy," he said, catching Flossie up
in his arms and calling her by his favorite nickname
for her. "Well, my fat fairy, I don't believe you will
have to worry about that. What I do think is that
you will have to be careful not to become impatient

with our new neighbors if they do not understand what you say or do."

"But they all speak English," Flossie told her father.

Mr. Bobbsey smiled and explained that the Castillios were used to living in a rather different way from the people in Lakeport. He understood their home was on a hacienda, a large farm, where it was extremely warm all the time; not chilly as it was in Lakeport today.

"Wouldn't it be nice to live in a place like that where the flowers bloom all the time?" he asked.

"And you could go swimming any day you wanted to," sighed Flossie.

Her father said that the Castillios probably would find the hustle and bustle of Lakeport life rather bewildering. He advised his small daughter and the other children not to try showing Mateo and Marina too many things at once. He smiled as he added:

"If I were you, I'd try to learn a lot from our new neighbors. No doubt they can tell you about things you never heard of."

At this moment the telephone rang. Mr. Bobbsey answered it and the children heard him say, "Yes, doctor."

Bert instantly realized that this was the physician his father had asked to go to Danny Rugg's home. He could hardly wait for the conversation to end.

"Is there really something wrong with Danny, Dad?" he asked when his father hung up.

Mr. Bobbsey puckered his brow. "I'm afraid Danny Rugg is a thoroughly unreliable youngster," he remarked. "According to the doctor there is nothing whatever the matter with Danny, although the boy insists that he was deliberately thrown from our truck."

"What will you do about it, Dad?" Bert asked.

"There is nothing more I can do now," Mr. Bobbsey replied. "But if Danny Rugg tries to make trouble, I certainly shall not let that young scamp get away with anything."

Dinah announced that luncheon was ready, and the Bobbsey family sat down to enjoy one of her delicious meals. Dinah rarely allowed the family to know ahead of time what the dessert was to be. Mrs. Bobbsey often laughed about that, saying her cook could think up more kinds of desserts than all the cookbooks put together.

Today was no exception. When Dinah carried in the last course, Freddie exclaimed:

"An Indian's hat!"

Sure enough, Dinah had arranged various colored ice creams on a platter in the form of an Indian headdress. The forehead band was made of raspberry ice. From this stuck up feathers of strawberry, vanilla, and chocolate. The tailpiece was a streamer of chocolate ice cream with small feathers of pink and white, and here and there a green feather of mint.

"It's so pretty I hate to spoil it," said Mrs. Bobbsey, as she picked up the serving spoon.

Freddie was more practical. "It will spoil itself by melting," he said.

A few minutes later he put a large spoonful of raspberry ice into his mouth. He ate a few more spoonfuls and then suddenly got off his chair. Assuming the position of an Indian in a dance, he began to run around the room, clapping his hands over his mouth and making a great noise. But his mother made him sit down immediately to finish his dessert.

"Don't try any of your war whooping at the Castillios' house," she warned her small son. Then with a smile, she added, "We wouldn't want them to think there are any uncivilized little boys in Lakeport who don't know how to behave at mealtime."

Freddie said no more, but he was sure that Mexican boys must like to play Indian too. He would ask Mateo when he saw him.

It was not until four o'clock that Mrs. Bobbsey decided it would be all right for her children to call on their new neighbors. She herself went with them. But when they rang the bell no one came to the door.

Freddie, impatient, put his finger on the button and held it there. The moment his mother discovered this she pulled his hand away. Still no one came to open the door.

"Oh, Mother," said Nan, "I guess they don't want to be friends with us, after all. Pedro must have told them about Waggo!"

At this instant they heard a loud scream inside the house!

CHAPTER IV

NEW FRIENDS

THE Bobbsey twins looked up at their mother, then at one another. What had happened in the home of their new neighbors?

The cry was not repeated, and Mrs. Bobbsey felt, since apparently they could do nothing to help, that they all should return home. She was somewhat puzzled by the fact that nobody had answered the doorbell.

Each of the twins in turn felt very curious about the whole matter. Fifteen minutes later Freddie and Flossie held a conference. They finally decided that maybe the Castillios had not answered the bell because they did not want so many callers at once.

"Perhaps if you and I go alone," suggested Flossie, "they'll let us in."

The small twins trotted across the street and rang the bell. But, as before, no one came to the door. Disappointed, the children left and returned to their back yard to play. Nan had gone to the store on an errand for her mother. Half an hour later, as she was returning, she met Bert coming from his friend Charlie Mason's house.

"Gee, Nan, I forgot to tell you about the traveling amusement park," he said. "I went to tell Charlie about it and see if he didn't want to go out and watch them build seats."

"Amusement park?" asked Nan, puzzled.

Bert told her about the showboat which was coming to Lakeport and how the owner set up a small amusement park wherever the boat docked.

"He brings everything even the bleachers. Dad's supplying the lumber for extra seats and for some small buildings they'll need—booths, I guess."

Nan was thrilled to hear about the boat which carried actors, actresses, a Ferris wheel, and other amusements. She said she hoped they could go to see the play on the boat. That would be just as much fun as taking in the amusements.

"Oh, look!" she cried out. "There are Mateo and Marina!"

"Well, what do you know about that!" exclaimed Bert. "They're waving to us to come over to their house!"

The twins hurried across the street. They were greatly surprised when Mateo said that the Castillios were disappointed when the Bobbsey children had not come over to see them!

"We did come," said Nan quickly. "Mother, too.

But no one opened the door when we rang the bell."

"That is very strange," said Mateo. "Perhaps it does not work."

The four children hurried up the porch steps. Mateo put his finger on the button. No one answered.

"I guess it doesn't work," laughed Nan. "You know, I thought you didn't want to be friends with us."

The Castillio children laughed too, and said this was furthest from their thoughts. They felt very strange and welcomed having new friends with whom to play. Marina suggested that Bert and Nan come into the house and see some pictures they had brought of their hacienda.

"Will you wait a minute while I get Flossie and Freddie?" Nan asked.

She ran home to get the younger twins, and took a moment to explain to her mother that the Castillios had asked them to come.

"Please tell Mrs. Castillio I'll call on her tomorrow," said Mrs. Bobbsey.

When the children entered the Castillio home the first person they saw was Anita.

"Duende!" she exclaimed, looking at Flossie.

Flossie smiled. "You called me that before. What does it mean?"

Anita told her that duendes were tiny little men who lived in the Mexican forests.

"They love to play tricks on people," she said. "Sometimes people can see them but usually they cannot."

"Oh!" said Flossie. "Am I like a little man? Daddy calls me his fat fairy," she explained. "But fairies are usually girls."

Marina spoke to Anita in Spanish and they both laughed merrily. Anita said:

"Flossie, you are so cute and you appear so suddenly that you are like a fairy. And in Mexico we have so many stories about the duendes I just called you that to tease you."

Flossie now wanted to hear more about the little elves that people said lived in the Mexican forests.

"How big are they and what do they do?" she asked.

"They are sometimes only twelve inches high," Mateo told her. "But they can be a trifle bigger. We usually think of them as having long white beards, and wearing green suits with pointed caps."

Freddie said they must look a little like Santa Claus's helpers, only they generally wore red suits. The Bobbsey twins each wished secretly that they might see a duende sometime.

"Now we will show you the pictures of our hacienda," said Mateo, and brought out a small book of color photographs.

The house was a large two-story structure of pink

stone. Flowering vines climbed all over it. There were many beautiful flower gardens and lovely walks which wound in and out among the gardens. Surrounding it all was a high, pink stone fence on which vines with red flowers grew. Against one wall was a large frog fountain. Water squirted from the mouth of the huge stone frog.

"The frog is very, very old," said Mateo.

"Is that why he's so fat?" Freddie asked.

The others laughed. Mateo said the frog had belonged to the Indians who lived in Mexico long before the Spanish people came there.

"The Indians were called Aztecs and they liked frogs. They used them to decorate some of their buildings. Our old fountain frog was found buried far down in the ground," Mateo explained.

"On your ha—ha ," Freddie stuttered, trying to say hacienda.

Mateo said the frog had been found near the pyramids, in a section of the country where it was somewhat cooler than where they lived.

The Bobbseys wondered what the pyramids were. Their new friend explained that they were huge mounds made of stone. Over a thousand years before, they had been built by the Aztecs to use in religious ceremonies.

"What else do you have in your country?" Flossie wanted to know.

The Castillio children smiled, and replied that they could not possibly tell about all the things in Mexico. The Bobbseys would have to come down there sometime and see for themselves.

The twins continued to look at the pictures of the hacienda. Outside the walls surrounding the house and garden was a little village of small thatch-roofed huts. In front of them cunning little Indian children were playing.

"The men who live in this village work for my father," said Marina.

One of the photographs showed a wooded mountain in the distance. Flossie asked if this was where the duendes lived. Anita, who came into the room at this moment, answered the question by saying she had a strong feeling that they did.

Nan began to count on her fingers. When the others inquired what she was doing, she explained that she was counting up all the things she had learned so far about Mexico; frogs, Aztecs, pyramids, and—

"You must learn to pronounce Mexico the Spanish way," Mateo interrupted. "Say it as if it were spelled May-hee-koh."

Right then and there the four Bobbsey twins started practicing the word. As they were doing this Mr. Castillio walked into the room. He smiled at the Bobbseys.

"I'm glad you are learning about my native land," he said. "Perhaps you will come down there some-time to visit us."

He was so friendly that Flossie was sure the Castillios were a very nice family. However, she was still puzzled by the scream she had heard and blurted out:

"You love your family, don't you, Mr. Castillio?"

"Indeed I do," he replied.

"And you wouldn't hurt any of them and make them scream?" the little girl asked him.

Mr. Castillio looked astonished and assured her he would not. Then he wanted to know why she had asked the question.

" 'Cause when we came to call on you the first time we heard someone scream," Flossie explained.

The Castillios seemed perplexed, but Anita broke into a broad grin. She told the Bobbseys that while she was standing in the kitchen Pedro had pushed a button in the wall. Then something had hit the top of her head and she had cried out.

"It was a board with legs on it," she said. "Maybe you can tell me what you do with it."

The children followed her into the kitchen. Anita pushed a button in the wall and out popped an iron-ing board. Nan told her what it was used for. Neither Anita nor any of the other Castillios had ever heard of ironing in a kitchen—all laundry work on their hacienda was done out of doors, and a table was used on which to iron.

"We might buy one of these ironing boards to send home," suggested Anita.

Mateo was not particularly interested in washing and ironing, so he suggested to Bert that they go outside. Through the window Mateo had seen a car standing in the driveway. The car belonged to the Martins, but they had left it for Mr. Castillio's use.

"Come on, Bert. Let's put the car away," Mateo said.

Bert thought the boy meant to push it, and felt this would be a pretty hard job. Mateo had no such intention. He hopped into the driver's seat and looked over the various gadgets.

"We might even go for a little ride," he remarked.

Bert was astonished. "You mean you know how to drive?" he asked.

"Of course," said Mateo. "Don't you?"

"Oh, no!" Bert replied. "I'll have to be several years older before I can get a license."

Mateo did not understand. When Bert explained that if anybody in Lakeport drove without a license he would be arrested, and that a person had to be sixteen years old to get a license there, Mateo decided he had better not take the car out into the street.

"I drive all over our hacienda," he remarked to Bert. "But we'll just put the car away now. Jump in," he added as he found the starter.

The engine roared. Mateo put it in gear and the car moved forward into the garage. Mateo put his foot on what he thought was the brake, but the automobile did not stop!

Suddenly there was a terrific crash. The car hit the rear wall of the wooden garage.

CHAPTER V

CHITO'S ADVENTURE

MR. Castillio was the first one out of the house to see what had caused the crash. Pedro was at his heels, and one by one the others rushed out after them.

What a sight met their eyes! The wrecked car had gone halfway through the back wall of the Martin garage!

Not a sound came from the two boys in the automobile. Mr. Castillio and Pedro rushed forward. Mateo and Bert lay crumpled on the front seat. Gently they were lifted out and laid on the grass.

"Oh, Bert!" cried Nan, kneeling beside her brother. His face was cut and bleeding.

"Mateo! Mateo!" wailed Marina when she saw the ugly gash on her brother's head.

Mr. Castillio and Pedro spoke swiftly in Spanish. In a moment Mrs. Castillio came from the house. She turned very white as she looked at the two boys on the ground.

The only one who seemed to know what to do was Freddie. Running as fast as he could to his own home, he shouted at the top of his lungs for his mother. She came rushing across the street, quickly introduced herself, and knelt down beside the two boys.

Anita had gone into the house, and now was bringing out a basin of cold water and some towels. Gently she swabbed the wound on Mateo's head, while Mrs. Bobbsey wiped the cut on her son's face. The shock of the cold water brought the two boys back to consciousness.

"Wh-what happened?" asked Bert weakly. Then he remembered. "Oh, yes, the car."

At these words Mateo recalled the awful thing he had done. He began to cry. His mother spoke to him soothingly in Spanish, and the Bobbseys guessed she was telling him it was more important that he was all right than that the car was damaged.

In a little while the two boys stood up. Mateo felt somewhat dizzy, but did not seem to be hurt. Bert fortunately was all right too, though the antiseptic which Anita brought and put on his cut face stung a great deal.

"This is made from herbs in my country," she explained to Mrs. Bobbsey. "It is an old Indian medicine."

It was decided that it would not be necessary to call a doctor, but both mothers thought it best for the boys to get to bed early. Accordingly, the Bobbseys started for home.

Mr. Castillio walked across the street with them. He said he was extremely sorry for what had happened, and hoped the Bobbseys would still be their friends. Mrs. Bobbsey assured him that the accident would make no difference. Furthermore, she would ask Mr. Bobbsey to see what he could do about rebuilding the wrecked wall. And she gave him the name of a man at a near-by service station who would do a good job of fixing the car.

"We did not plan to have such an exciting time in Lakeport our first day," said Mr. Castillio. "But at least it has given us a chance to find out what nice neighbors we have in the Bobbsey family."

Bert was hustled into bed and given a light supper. He insisted he felt all right, but both his mother and Dinah thought he should rest. The next morning, however, he was up early. Seeing the service-station wrecker across the street, he dressed quickly and went over to the Castillio garage.

Two men were examining the car. Its headlights were smashed, the radiator pushed in, the windshield shattered, and both front tires were punctured.

"It's amazing what these things can stand," said one of the men. "It won't cost as much to fix her up as it will to fix the garage. Whew! What a mess this is! Those boys were lucky that they weren't badly hurt."

Bert watched as the wrecker came into the drive-

way, and pulled the battered car out of the garage.
Then the men hoisted up the front end of it onto
the wrecker. As Bert saw them go down the street,
he realized what a lucky escape he and Mateo had
had. Wondering how Mateo felt this morning, he
knocked on the door.

Pedro answered. He was glad to learn that Bert
was all right. He said Mateo was not awake yet
but was sure that he was all right, too.

"Please tell him to come over to my house when
he gets up," said Bert. "Another boy and I are going
down to the amusement park. Maybe Mateo would
like to go along with us."

Pedro said he would tell him, and Bert went home.
As he came into the back yard, he found Flossie hanging doll clothes on the line. Since it was a beautiful
day, Dinah had decided Flossie should do her laundry work outdoors, and Flossie thought it would be
fun because that was the way many people in Mexico
cleaned their clothes.

"I'm playing I'm living on the Castillios' haci—"
Flossie told Bert. She could not pronounce that word
"hacienda."

"You'd better keep Waggo out of the way," Bert
suggested. "Look what he's done to your little tub
of water."

Flossie turned to look. That naughty dog! With
his nose and front paws he had tipped over the tub

and spilled the water on the ground. Now he had
the cake of soap in his mouth and was running off
with it. The little girl ran after him. Waggo did not
like the taste of the soap, and a moment later he
dropped it to the ground.

Flossie went on with her work. As Bert entered
the house, his friend Charlie Mason arrived. Charlie
wanted to leave for the amusement park at once, but
Bert said they must wait for Mateo. In a short time
he came over. Bert introduced him to Charlie and
then the boys hurried away.

Nan, looking after them, felt rather envious. She
had finished all her chores, and there seemed to be
nothing to do. Then she smiled.

"I know what I'll do," she decided. "I'll go over
to the Castillios and ask them if I can take Chito out
and show him to my friends."

She slipped on a sweater, and then went across the
street. Mr. and Mrs. Castillio had gone out with
Marina, but Pedro and Anita said they were sure it
would be all right for Nan to take the little dog out,
provided she kept him warm.

"I'll take good care of him," she promised, lifting
Chito from his basket.

She tucked him inside her sweater, but the tiny
little dog slid right down through as the sweater
stretched. Nan caught him just as he was about to
fall to the floor. His little claws had pulled several
strands of the wool.

"Oh!" cried Anita. "Your pretty sweater is ruined!"

"I guess Mother can fix it," Nan replied, not worried. "But I'm glad Chito didn't hit the floor. I'd better go home and put my jacket on, so he can't fall out."

She skipped across the street with Chito and got the jacket from her bedroom. As she reached the first floor again, Nan met Dinah in the hall. The cook threw up her hands in surprise.

"Lawsy me!" she exclaimed. "What yo' got dere?"

The little dog did not move. He stared straight at her with his big eyes wide open.

Dinah relaxed. She had thought for a moment that what Nan was carrying was alive, but now she was sure it was merely some new toy which she had not seen before. But as she looked, the "toy" suddenly bobbed its head and barked at her. Dinah fell back a step.

"Oh, mah goodness!" she cried out. "It's a livin' critter after all. Some kind of a deer? But I nevah seed a deer before what could bark."

Nan giggled at Dinah's mistake. She took the dog out of her jacket and the Negro woman laughed until she trembled all over.

"Now dat beats all," she remarked. "A dog wif'-out hair what looks lak a dwarf deer when his body don't show."

Shaking her head, she went off. Nan hurried down the street to the house of her friend Nellie Parks. Nellie was delighted with the Mexican dog and was almost as amazed at his looks as Dinah had been. She begged to hold the little animal. Nan warned her about keeping him warm, so she, too, put on a jacket.

The two girls walked into the business section of Lakeport on their way to call on another girl who lived across town. Every few feet some passer-by would stop them to look at Chito. As they went by a photographer's studio, Nan said:

"Let's go in and have Chito's picture taken."

"Have you enough money with you?" Nellie reminded her. "I can give you a quarter."

"I have a quarter, too," said Nan. "I'll ask the man if he can make a picture for fifty cents."

Ordinarily the photographer would have charged much more, but he was very much taken with the little Mexican dog, so he laughingly agreed to make two pictures for fifty cents. He took one of Nan holding Chito, and then said he would like to take one of the dog alone. The girls stood in a corner of the studio, trying to make Chito keep still on the stool while the man adjusted his lights.

It was evident that Chito did not like having his picture taken. Half a second after the photographer had snapped the dog's picture, Chito made a leap to the back of the room and disappeared under a curtain.

"Oh, gracious!" cried Nan, dashing after him.

She pulled the curtain aside. Before her was a room filled with bottles, pans, and other photographic equipment. Chito was not there.

"Where could he have gone?" Nan exclaimed, growing worried.

"I guess he went out through that hole," said the photographer, pointing to a small opening in the rear wall of the room.

The man turned, opened another door from the studio, and raced to the back. Nan and Nellie ran after him. Chito was not in sight!

A door leading to an alley was open. Assuming that Chito had run out there, the three raced out to the alley. But the little dog was not there.

"Oh, what shall I do?" cried Nan desperately.

CHAPTER VI

THE AMUSEMENT PARK

TEARS rolled down Nan's cheeks. She had broken her promise to Pedro and Anita to take good care of Chito. Not only was he gone, but perhaps at this very moment he was lying hurt somewhere.

"We must do something," she told the photographer urgently.

The man patted her shoulder and said, "Even tiny dogs know how to take care of themselves pretty well. Now let's just think this thing out. Chito is too small to have gone very far in such a short time."

"Then maybe he's still inside," Nan exclaimed, taking heart.

She hurried back into the building, followed by the others. With Nellie and the photographer, Nan began an intensive hunt in the rear room. They looked behind piles of picture frames, stacks of cardboard, rolls of paper, heaps of newspapers, and even pulled out several boxes. Chito was not behind any of them; nor was he inside anything.

Nan became discouraged. Deciding next to search the developing room into which Chito had fled, she went back into the studio.

"R-r-r-r!" said a tiny voice.

Nan could hardly believe her eyes. On the stool sat Chito, just as if he were having his picture taken.

Nan was so happy to see him she did not know whether to hug him in delight, or scold him for being so mischievous. Grabbing him up she called to the others. They were greatly relieved to see Chito, especially the photographer, who had felt responsible for the dog's disappearance. He told Nan the pictures would be ready in a couple of days if she would stop in for them.

As she and Nellie walked home, Nan asked her friend if she had heard about the traveling amusement park that was coming to Lakeport. Nellie had heard nothing about it, and was excited to learn about the showboat as well.

"Bert and Charlie and Mateo went out to the grounds this morning," Nan said. "I'll bet they're having a lot of fun watching the carpenters."

The three boys were indeed having fun. Only two men had come to put up the extra seats so when the boys offered to help, their offer was quickly accepted. They helped to carry the boards which the men set in place and nailed down. Within an hour a great deal of work had been accomplished, and now one end of the bleachers was nearly complete.

"How'd you fellows like to paint the seat numbers on?" one of the workmen asked.

"Sure thing," Bert replied.

He opened a can of black paint, found a brush, and got busy. In the meantime Charlie and Mateo went on carrying boards. They were just starting on a new pile when around the corner of the street appeared Freddie Bobbsey.

The small boy, having heard where his brother had gone, could not resist the temptation to follow him. Freddie had asked first one person, then another, to find out where the amusement park was to be. For several seconds he stood watching what was going on. He would have loved to help Bert with the painting! But he knew that his brother would not let him do this.

"But I could help with the boards," thought Freddie. "I could climb up to the top of that pile and push them down to Charlie."

The others were so busy working that no one noticed Freddie as he hurried across the lot and scampered up the pile of boards. Just as he reached the top, Charlie and Mateo turned back from the bleachers.

"Hey! Look who's here!" cried Charlie, adding, "Freddie, you'd better get down."

"I want to help!" Freddie replied firmly. "I want to—"

Freddie got no further in what he intended to say. Suddenly the pile of boards began to quiver. First there was a scraping sound, then a resounding crash as the lumber toppled over. The small boy slid with them, landing on the ground with one of the boards on top of him!

Bert had turned around when he heard Charlie cry out. Now he jumped from the bleachers and rushed toward his brother. Charlie, Mateo, and the two workmen also hurried to Freddie and quickly lifted up the board.

Freddie tried to stand, but his legs gave way under him and down he sat. He put one hand to his head and another on his knee.

"That—that's all that hurts," he said, trying to hold back the tears. He wanted so much to be brave, even though the breath had been knocked out of him for a moment.

"We'd better take you right home," said one of the workmen. "I'll get my car."

"But I don't want to go home," argued Freddie. "I just came."

The man decided that this was no place for a small boy, and told Freddie he could come back in a few days when the amusement park was ready.

"Here's something for you," he said, taking a ticket from his pocket and handing it to Freddie. "A fellow gave this to me but you can use it."

Freddie forgot all about being scared or hurt.

Here was an admission ticket to the amusement park. "Oh, boy!" he exclaimed. "This is swell! Thank you, sir."

The workman drove all the boys home. Freddie begged Bert not to tell the family what he had done. Bert agreed but could not keep Freddie from having a large bump on his forehead. But when the other members of the Bobbsey family questioned him about it, he merely said:

"Can't a fellow get a bump once in a while?"

When Mr. Bobbsey came home that evening he had news for the twins. The showboat was going to dock the next morning! He would take them down there before going to his office if they would like to see it. And would they like to see it!

"May I take Marina with us?" Flossie asked her father.

"And Mateo too?" Bert requested.

Mr. Bobbsey laughed. "We've had seven people in my five-passenger car before, so I guess we can do it again. Suppose you telephone the Castillios' house and find out if the children would like to go."

Mateo and Marina were delighted, but when they joined the Bobbseys in the crisp early morning the following day, Marina yawned and remarked, "Do people in Lakeport always get up so early? On our hacienda we sleep much later."

Nan told her that they got up even earlier when

school was in session. Just now they were having a vacation.

"Where do you go to school?" Flossie inquired of her new neighbors.

The Castillio children smiled and said they went to school right at home. They were taught by a tutor who lived on the hacienda.

"We really have three teachers," Mateo remarked. "One teaches us from books. Another is our music teacher. The third teaches us to dance."

The Bobbsey twins learned that both children could play several instruments; the piano, guitar, and violin.

"That's wonderful," said Nan. "Did you bring a guitar and a violin with you?"

"No," Mateo replied. "We had too much baggage as it was, and we want to take many things home with us from the United States."

Nan decided that she would find a guitar somewhere so she could hear her new friends play. She asked what else they learned from the tutors, and was amazed at the answer. The Mexican children not only studied all the subjects which Nan and Bert had at school, but Marina also was being taught to sew and embroider, and Mateo was an expert horseman. Both children could speak several languages.

Flossie was thoughtful for several minutes. Then she said, "I believe I'm wasting my time. I ought to give up playing with dolls and learn to sew and speak Spanish and do lots of other things."

Her father smiled. "I shouldn't want my fat fairy to give up playing with dolls," he said, "but I'm glad to hear that you're going to study a little harder."

Nan remarked that she had heard the Castillio family speak very little Spanish since they had arrived. "Surely you speak Spanish among yourselves?" she asked.

Marina said they always spoke Spanish in the house, but they did not think it polite to do so when there were people present who did not know Spanish. That was why they always spoke English when the twins were around. The Bobbseys decided that they had never known nicer children.

By this time they had reached the road which led to the grounds of the traveling amusement park. In the distance they could see a boat steaming up to a dock on the river.

"Oh, let's hurry," Freddie urged. "We don't want to miss anything."

They arrived just as long, heavy ropes were being thrown to the dock. Presently the men on shore had the steamer securely tied. It was called the *Sea Gull*. A gangplank was hoisted and the captain came ashore. He was a plump, jolly-looking man.

Freddie nudged his father, wanting to know if this man was the chief of the Ferris wheel. Mr. Bobbsey

smiled and said he would find out. Approaching the
captain, he inquired if he were the owner of the showboat.

"Yes," was the reply. "I'm also the captain, and
I act in the shows, and I can run any of the amusements if we're shorthanded."

The children thought this was remarkable, but
none of it seemed so remarkable as his name. The
man said he was Captain Friday Night. He explained that he had been given his mother's maiden
name, which was Freiday. His father's name was
Knight. But the captain had found it a nuisance to
have to spell his name to people, so now he simply
signed himself Captain Friday Night.

"My name has brought me good luck," he said.
"So every Friday I have a special show."

The children wanted to hear what it was. The
captain replied by inviting them to come on board to
meet the actors who took part in it.

"I have some very, very little folks in my show,"
he told them. "They are no bigger than you," he
added, looking directly at Flossie and Freddie, "but
they are old men."

The small twins wondered excitedly whether they
could be duendes!

CHAPTER VII

STRANGE PEOPLE

THE children trooped on board the *Sea Gull* after Captain Friday Night. He led them into the dining hall of the showboat. There were two long tables in the room. At one sat only men. Captain Night said they were the workers in the amusement park.

At the other table sat both men and women having breakfast. These were the actors and actresses who performed in the ship's theater. Up at the far end of the table, on high stools, sat six little men. Their faces were small, their hands were small, and even the dishes in front of them were smaller than those in front of the others.

"Company," said Captain Night in a loud voice, "I want you to meet some people from Lakeport. This is Mr. Bobbsey, who supplied the lumber for our new bleachers. He has a most remarkable family —two sets of twins, if you please. And this boy and girl," he added, pointing to Mateo and Marina, "are visiting here from Mexico."

"Most unusual," said one of the actors, slowly rising to his feet.

As the children looked at him, they wondered what was happening. As he got out of his chair he kept going up and up and up toward the ceiling. They wondered if he was ever going to stop.

"My giant," announced Captain Night with a hearty laugh. "He always enjoys surprising children who come to visit our showboat."

Flossie took hold of the captain's sleeve and whispered, "Those little men at the end of the table, are they duendes?"

"Are they what?" the captain asked her.

"Did they come from a forest in Mexico?" Flossie went on.

"Yes, they did," he replied. It was his turn to be surprised. "How in the world did you know that?" he asked.

Flossie had no chance to answer, because at that moment the children saw a sight which made chills run down their spines. The hair on top of one man's head was jumping up and down! Flossie grabbed her sister's hand and held it very tightly, as the man with the bobbing scalp grinned at her.

"It must be a wig," Nan explained, no longer frightened at the strange sight.

It *was* a wig, and the man who wore it could wiggle his forehead and scalp so that the artificial hair danced about on his head.

"Does he do that in your show?" Freddie asked Captain Night.

"Oh, yes," the captain replied. "He's in one of the side shows."

"And what do the little men do?" Nan inquired.

The captain said they had two different acts; a funny one and a scary one. He described the scary one.

"It is a forest scene," he said. "The little men are hard at work chopping trees and making toys from them, when suddenly a big storm comes up."

"Real water?" Freddie wanted to know.

"Indeed, yes," said the captain. "But the poor little men are not able to get out of the rain, because the thunder becomes a great giant who orders them to work for him. And the lightning plays around, making them jump from place to place, so they must obey."

"Poor men," said Flossie sympathetically. "They must get awfully wet."

The captain laughed. He told them there was only a little bit of real water. The rest was magic rain made by a moving-picture projector.

"There's only one thing the matter with the act," Captain Night informed his visitors. "One or another of my little men is always becoming ill, and then I can't have the show because all of them have to be in it."

"Why do you only have it on Fridays?" Bert wanted to know.

"Because of my name, and because during school-time the children can come that night. The show is mostly for children. However," the captain went on, "we're going to have two shows while we're in Lakeport. One tomorrow night and one on Friday."

At this point Freddie pulled his ticket to the amusement park from his pocket. He inquired if this would admit him to the play on the showboat as well.

"I'm afraid not, little man," Captain Night replied. "But the admission is not expensive."

Mr. Bobbsey said he would like to get some reserved seats at once. On a chance that Mr. and Mrs. Castillio would give permission for their children to attend the performance also, he bought two extra tickets. He then remarked that it was high time for him to be getting to his office and that they must leave. The children did not want to leave, and the boys begged to stay and watch the equipment being unloaded from the showboat and erected on the amusement park grounds.

"I'll tell you what I'll do," Mr. Bobbsey said. "Perhaps Pedro and Anita would like to come back here with you. I'll let them use my car."

Flossie held up her fingers and began to count. In a moment she said:

"That'll make eight people, Daddy. Can you get

eight people in where only five are supposed to be?"

Her father smiled and said that was the best he could do in the way of transportation, so the eight would have to squeeze in somehow.

Satisfied, the children climbed into Mr. Bobbsey's car and were driven back to their homes. Mrs. Castillio said it would be all right for Pedro and Anita to accompany the children and soon the group drove back to the park. The children were glad that very little had been done yet.

What a busy place it was! Some workmen were carrying parts of the Ferris wheel from the boat. Others were stringing wires for lights around the grounds. Tents were being put up here and there.

As the children watched, one man came from the *Sea Gull* carrying a small wooden lion under his arm. Behind him came another workman with a zebra. Soon a small merry-go-round was set up. Immediately Flossie was tired and had to sit down on one of the animals. She whispered to Freddie and Marina and the three climbed onto a lion, a zebra, and a camel.

"How about a ride?" someone behind them asked.

They turned around to find the giant smiling at them. The tall man stepped across the platform to the center where the machinery was. He pushed a button, clicked a switch, and twirled a little handle. A moment later the merry-go-round began to move and the organ music started to play.

"This is fun!" shouted Freddie.

Flossie and Marina thought so too, but only for half a minute. Suddenly the merry-go-round began to go faster and faster. The children clung tightly to the animals' heads, but they felt as if at any moment they themselves would be flung off.

The giant was trying frantically to stop the machine. Unfortunately the men who had set up the merry-go-round had not completed their work, and the giant could not stop it. Realizing the danger to the children, he decided to rescue them.

Stepping onto the whirling platform, he grabbed Flossie in his arms and leaped to the ground. Willing hands took the little girl from him. Then the giant jumped back on the merry-go-round, seized Marina, and jumped off with her. Pedro and Anita cried out in relief.

Poor Freddie, left alone, was fearful that he was not going to be rescued in time. He was growing dizzy and was sure he could not hold on another second. Everything began to swim before his eyes. Gradually he let go the zebra's neck.

Then two things happened at once. He was pulled off the wooden animal by the giant, and the merry-go-round began to slow down. Captain Night, having seen what was happening, had shut off the electric current.

The small Bobbsey twins and Marina were safe!

Nan, Bert, and Mateo crowded around them, as well as Pedro, Anita, and the various workmen. The giant, perspiring and trembling, flopped down on the ground. He felt relieved, of course, that nothing had happened to the children, but he had had such a fright he wondered if he ever would get over it. The poor fellow apologized over and over again.

Even the actors and actresses, having heard shouts, came running from the showboat. When the twins saw the six little men coming, they were so amused they quite forgot what had happened to them. The midgets, for that is what they really were, made funny faces and did somersaults to entertain the children so they would completely forget the episode of the merry-go-round.

Nan asked the little men their names, but when she heard them, they were so long and so unpronounceable she knew she never could remember them. She asked if they would mind if she called them something easy.

"What would you suggest?" said the smallest man in a high squeaky voice. The top of his head came only to her shoulder, so she sat down on the ground to talk to him.

"How about Mr. A, and Mr. B, and Mr. C?" Nan suggested.

The jolly little fellow laughed. His laugh reminded

the children of the tinkle of a bell with a slight crack in it.

"Suppose you name us now," he said. "We'll line up and you can decide which letters of the alphabet we'll be."

Nan thought for a moment. Then she had an inspiration. "Captain Night says you came from a Mexican forest. Your names together will spell Mexico. You'll be Mr. M." Pointing to another little man near her, she said, "You'll be Mr. E. And this one will be Mr. X," she went on.

After each one had received his title, the midgets went back to the *Sea Gull,* because they had work to do to get ready for the show the next day. They invited the Bobbsey and Castillio children to come over to watch them. Pedro and Anita felt they should go home, but their young charges begged so hard to stay that they finally relented.

One by one they went up the gangplank and made their way to the ship's theater.

CHAPTER VIII

A MYSTERY

UNKNOWN to the Bobbseys and their friends, Danny Rugg had come down to the traveling amusement park to watch the proceedings. The boy knew he would not be welcome if he joined the twins. But he was very envious of the attention they were getting. Furthermore, he wondered who the strange children were who were with them.

"Maybe I can find out," he told himself.

When he overheard the invitation from the little men, Danny decided to follow the others onto the showboat. Fortunately for him, no one paid any attention to him. When the twins and their friends went into the ship's theater, he slid into a seat at the back.

But Danny Rugg could not sit still nor behave for very long at one time. For a few minutes he watched the little men up on the stage repairing the scenery for their set. He was intrigued by the small hammers, saws, and screw drivers they used.

"Bert, would you and Mateo like to come up

here?" Danny heard one of the little men ask in a squeaky voice.

Danny's face turned red with jealousy. He wanted to go up on the stage, but he did not dare join the others because he was sure he would be put off the boat.

"I'll sneak around back," he decided.

Going out the rear door of the theater, he walked down a corridor. No one was about. Danny found a side door to the stage, opened it, and tiptoed up the steps leading to the back of the stage. He was hidden by the scenery.

Danny wondered how he could get some action. Almost before he knew what he was doing, he pushed over a make-believe tree, and dodged out of sight. Then he heaved over a wooden cave. Running across the back of the stage, he knocked down the front of a make-believe hut.

What confusion there was on the stage! The little men who had been hit by the scenery cried out in pain. The tree whacked Mr. M a resounding blow on the back. Mr. X found himself on the floor beneath the wooden cave.

"Who did that?" yelled Pedro, jumping onto the stage and lifting up the pieces of scenery one by one.

Nobody knew. Danny's selfish desire for fun had turned into misfortune for others. Scared, he ran up the corridor of the ship, went down the gangplank as fast as he possibly could, and hastened toward home, hoping no one had seen him.

Meanwhile, back on the stage, little Mr. M and Mr. X were being carried to the stateroom where they slept. Bert had rushed off to telephone to a doctor who lived near by.

The Bobbseys and the Castillios felt very bad that the two midgets had been hurt. They were sure that the scenery had been pushed over deliberately, and now the older children began to look for evidence as to who had done it. After a thorough search Nan found a clue. On the floor was a crumpled piece of paper. It seemed to be a grocery list and at the top was scrawled in pencil the name Barron's.

"If this fell out of the pocket of the person who knocked over the scenery," said Nan, "maybe we can find out from Barron's store who left this order."

"You're a very clever child," spoke up Captain Night, who had joined in the search.

The visitors left at once, saying they hoped the little men had not been seriously hurt, and would be able to be in the show the next evening. The children added that they would come early as they did not want to miss anything.

Pedro and Anita took all the children home except Bert and Nan. The twins stopped off at Barron's grocery store to find out what they could about the piece of paper Bert now had in his pocket. They went

directly to Mr. Barron himself and explained what
they wanted to know. The shopkeeper was very glad
to help. He himself had not taken the order listed on
the paper, but he asked the clerks in his shop about
it. One of them said:

"That order looks familiar. Let me see. Oh, I remember it especially because it had tartar sauce on it
and I hate tartar sauce." The clerk thought hard.
"I'm sure the order was not delivered. Someone came
in here and took it. Yes, it was a boy."

"What did he look like?" Bert asked quickly.

The young man scratched his head. "I'm sorry, but
I can't remember. I can tell you this, though. He had
on a pair of shoes that squeaked louder than any
shoes I've ever heard in my life. I finally asked him
if he had a mouse in them, and he said 'Go ask Mr.
Temple.' "

The Bobbsey twins thanked the clerk and Mr. Barron for their trouble. Then they set off excitedly for
Temple's shoe store to find out what boy was wearing
a squeaky pair of shoes from the shop. Nan giggled,
saying she doubted that Mr. Temple would admit
any of his shoes squeaked, and that they would have
to be very tactful.

They were amazed, upon entering the shop, to
hear a woman speaking about the very subject which
they had in mind. She was holding a pair of boys'
slightly worn shoes, and demanding her money back.

Mr. Temple, instead of being annoyed, was very polite.

"I'm extremely sorry, madam, that you have had trouble with these," he said. "A poor shipment of these shoes came in. If I can locate all the people who bought them I shall be very glad to replace the shoes."

This was Bert and Nan's opportunity. Going up to Mr. Temple, Nan remarked, "We'd like to help you find those people. It's very important for us to find out who one of them is."

"Well, well," smiled Mr. Temple, "I'll be glad of your help. If you'll just sit down a moment I'll talk to you about it."

The twins waited until he had given the woman another pair of shoes, and then they explained how they were trying to trace someone who had caused an accident on the showboat. Mr. Temple said he was very glad to be of assistance to them in trying to solve the mystery. He looked through his records, and found that he had the names of three persons to whom he had sold the squeaky shoes.

"Their names are Bill Smith, Ray Brown, and Danny Rugg," he told the twins.

"Danny Rugg!" exclaimed Bert and Nan together.

"You know him?" Mr. Temple inquired.

"We sure do," Bert replied. "And I'll bet he's the one who caused the accident."

Mr. Temple advised the Bobbseys to proceed with care. After all, their evidence was pretty roundabout, and he felt they should not accuse Danny without first being very sure.

"Thank you, sir," said Bert. "We'll be very careful."

Outside the store once more the twins wondered what they should do. They decided to go at once to Danny's house. They found him playing in the back yard. As they approached him a frightened look came over the young bully's face.

"Why did you come here?" he asked them quickly.

"To do you a favor," replied Bert.

Danny was suspicious at once. His eyes opened wide when the twins told him that they had been in Temple's shoe store and heard about certain boys who had received squeaky shoes.

"Mr. Temple wants to exchange them for good shoes," Nan said.

"Well, all right, thanks," said Danny grudgingly and started for the house.

But Bert was not ready to let him go. "Say, I heard a funny thing down at Barron's store," he said. "Nan and I were in there, and one of the clerks was telling us a joke."

"What was it?" Danny wanted to know.

"The man told us about a boy who was in there yesterday. His shoes squeaked so loudly the fellow asked him if he had a mouse in them. Ha! Ha!" roared Bert.

"Imagine a mouse in your shoes." Nan giggled. "The clerk didn't know who the boy was, but he said he made a good answer."

"He did?" exclaimed Danny, his eyes sparkling. "That's because I'm so smart."

"You!" said Bert, trying not to show his excitement.

"Sure," said Danny. "I was that boy." As he said this, he swelled out his chest. Then he continued toward the house. "Sure, I was that bright boy," he said.

Nan and Bert looked at each other. They knew now that Danny was responsible for the accident on the showboat! But the twins wondered what to do about it. As they stood thinking, Danny disappeared into the house.

"Oh, Bert, what shall we do?" Nan asked. "We mustn't let Danny get away with this!"

CHAPTER IX

THE BOBBSEY ELVES

NAN and Bert need not have worried about having to do anything in regard to Danny. The mean boy suddenly realized why they had come. At once he became both angry and frightened. While they were standing outside his house, still trying to decide what to do, he rushed down the porch steps and confronted them.

"You didn't see me do it!" he cried out in a loud voice. "You can't prove anything!"

Now, unfortunately for Danny, his mother at that minute came to a second-floor window. Hearing her son's words, she stopped to listen.

"It doesn't make any difference who saw you. You hurt two people and you've got to do something about it," declared Bert.

"Who'd I hurt?" said the boy. "That scenery wasn't heavy."

Nan said perhaps the scenery would not have hurt a large person, but that two of the little men who had been knocked over were no bigger than children.

"Maybe they can't be in the show tomorrow," the girl went on.

Mrs. Rugg decided the matter sounded serious. She hurried down the stairs and came outside.

"What is this all about?" she demanded of her son.

Danny did not want to tell her, but when the boy realized she already knew something about it, he owned up to his bad behavior. Mrs. Rugg, shocked, said the two of them would go at once to the *Sea Gull* and do what they could to make amends.

The Bobbsey twins went on home. Freddie and Flossie asked eagerly if they had found out who had pushed over the scenery. When they heard it was Danny, they were not surprised.

"Oh, I hope those duende men will be all right tomorrow," said Flossie. "Captain Friday Night said he needs all his little people in the show or he can't have it."

Flossie's wish about the midgets did not come true, but, because of this, a very unusual thing happened to her and Freddie. Directly after luncheon the following day the Bobbseys' doorbell rang, and when Dinah opened the door Captain Night stood there. He said that he wished to consult Mrs. Bobbsey on a very important matter.

"I'se sorry, sir," said Dinah, "but she's not at home."

The captain of the *Sea Gull* looked disappointed. Then he asked if any of the twins were there. Upon learning that they all were at home, he asked to see them. As they trooped into the living room he caught Flossie by one hand and Freddie by the other.

"Let me get a good look at you," he said. Then with a grin he added, "Yes, you'll do very nicely."

"We'll do very nicely for what?" Flossie questioned him, puzzled.

The man said that his two injured midgets would not be able to perform that evening. He did not want to cancel the show. And he thought perhaps Flossie and Freddie, with a little practice, could take the parts of the elves who had been hurt.

"Oh—h—h!" exclaimed Flossie.

"Wow!" yelled Freddie and did a somersault. Then he asked, "Could I use my fire engine?"

Captain Friday Night said the act did not call for a fire engine, but that it did require some somersaults, and he was glad to see that Freddie knew how to do them.

"If you children would like to be in the show you ought to come down at once and practice with my little men," he said. "Can you get in touch with your mother or father and get permission?"

Nan, excited, flew to the telephone and called up

Mr. Bobbsey. When he heard about Captain Night's request, he laughed merrily. "My twins have been a number of things," he said, "but never midgets. So my little fireman and my fat fairy are going to be elves tonight. Nan, you and Bert had better go with them. Tell Captain Night I will pick you all up on my way home from the office."

On their way to the showboat the small twins asked so many questions that the captain tried to answer three or four at once. The main thing that worried the children was how he was going to make Flossie look like a man.

The captain laughed. "In show business a little grease paint and a wig can do wonders," he said.

He was right. Half an hour later, Bert and Nan, sitting in the theater, hardly recognized their small brother and sister as they came out on the stage. They had on one-piece green suits, and over their shoes were little green slippers with long, curled-up toes. Flossie's blonde curls were tightly tucked under a high, pointed bonnet which was buckled under her chin. The bonnet was the same color as the suit. The skin on her face and hands had been darkened. Freddie was dressed the same way.

"I can hardly tell them apart," Nan whispered to Bert.

"And they do look like the other little men," said

Bert, "except not quite so old. They look as if they might be the sons of the others."

By this time the act on the stage was beginning. Freddie somersaulted out of the left wing and landed in front of Mr. C. He sat there grinning. Mr. C pretended to whack him with a stick to make him get up and go to work.

The whole act was full of fun. The elves were trying to build a hut, but everything was going wrong. One of them rolled out a keg of nails. It bumped right into Mr. M who really was Flossie, and over she tumbled. She stood the keg up, climbed on top, and started a little dance.

But Mr. O, who was the boss of the workmen, made her get down and pick up a hammer. She ran over to the hut and pretended to pound a nail into the wall, but suddenly the hammer flew backward out of her hand and landed in the face of Mr. E. He made believe he was badly hurt and fell over—but since the hammer was made of rubber, of course, he was not hurt one bit.

All this time Freddie had been busy helping two of the elves saw a log in half. Just as they finished, he looked around and—bang! The log fell right on his toes!

Freddie danced around on one foot and Nan and Bert almost felt sorry for him. They knew, of course, that his injury was faked. The log was made of rubber. In fact, it was two logs put together, and Freddie had not even gone to the trouble of sawing it at all!

When the play was over, Bert and Nan clapped loudly. They thought their brother and sister had done very well, but Captain Night coming from backstage said it could be greatly improved. He made the small twins go over and over their parts, until Nan was afraid they would be so tired they could not be in the show that evening. She insisted they rest.

"You're right," said Captain Friday Night. "They can take naps in a couple of the staterooms."

Now Freddie and Flossie, had they been at home, probably would have objected to taking naps, but the idea of sleeping on a showboat was so different they trotted off willingly to the bunks. Freddie was actually going to sleep on the captain's bed!

When Mr. Bobbsey arrived at five-thirty he found his small twins sound asleep. Presently they awakened, refreshed and ready for their evening's adventure.

"How about letting them stay right here?" Captain Night suggested. "We're going to have a light supper—we never eat much before a show," he said. "I'm sure the menu will be suitable for your children."

The twins' father agreed to let them stay. Knowing that they would have to be made up again for the evening performance, it seemed a good idea.

It was not often that Nan and Bert were envious of their young brother and sister, but this time they wished they, too, might be staying. They went home with their father, however, had their own supper, and dressed for the trip to the showboat and the amusement park.

"My goodness!" exclaimed Nan suddenly as she combed her hair. "I almost forgot about Marina and Mateo."

The Castillio children were to go with them. Before the twins were ready, the Mexican children arrived at the Bobbsey house. They were excited to hear about Freddie and Flossie being in the show.

"Maybe we shouldn't have told you," said Nan. "I'm sure you'll never recognize them."

"I believe it will be more fun this way," smiled Marina sweetly.

She could hardly wait to see the performance of the little men. There were three other acts which came before it; and, though the children enjoyed them all, they did not think any of them so funny or so clever as the one of the hard-working elves, who had such a difficult time getting their cabin built. After the act was over, Captain Night came out on the stage and presented Mr. M and Mr. X, but he didn't call them by these names. He gave them the long unpronounceable titles which were the real names of the midgets. Then, at a signal, Flossie and Freddie pulled off their pointed green caps. The audience gasped.

"And now let me introduce two of your neighbors," smiled Captain Night. "The son and daughter of Mr. and Mrs. Richard Bobbsey."

All through the audience were murmurs of "Oh, aren't they cute!" "Oh, I never dreamed such a thing!" "They certainly played their parts well."

Mrs. Bobbsey was very proud of the twins, but she felt that after so much excitement, they should go home. She promised they might come down to the amusement park the next afternoon. Mr. Bobbsey drove them home, and Dinah hurried them off to bed.

In the meantime, the other four children walked around the grounds of the amusement park. The boys were amazed that so much entertainment could be crowded into a small space and that everything had been set up so quickly. Of all the attractions, the Castillio children were most interested in the Ferris wheel. They had never seen one before and were eager to ride on it with the twins.

"Will you sit very still if I let you go up?" Mrs. Bobbsey asked.

She would have gone with them, but only two persons were allowed to ride in each car. They all promised, so she purchased tickets. The ride included three complete turns of the big wheel.

The Mexican children were very much excited. On the very first trip up, the machine stopped to take on a couple of passengers. The children were at the very top of the Ferris wheel. They not only could look over the amusement park but could see the lights of the town of Lakeport.

"I wonder if I could find my house," said Nan.

But before she could find it, the Ferris wheel began to move. Around they went for the second time. Then, on the third trip, the girls' car stopped at the very top. The boys were just a little below.

"Bert," Nan called to her brother, "can you see our house?"

The boy strained his eyes trying to see the Bobbsey home. He pointed where he thought it was. Nan was sure it was further to the left. The friendly little argument lasted several minutes, and they did not realize that the Ferris wheel had not moved.

"I would like to get out now," said Marina. "I want to ride on something else."

But still the Ferris wheel did not move. The children looked down. They could see men below talking excitedly and waving their arms about. One of them was working at a lever. He seemed to be trying to pull it forward, but it would not move.

Mrs. Bobbsey, standing near by, became alarmed. She walked over to hear what the men were saying. To her horror she learned the Ferris wheel was stuck!

Her twins and the Castillio children were trapped in the air!

CHAPTER X

A RESCUE

IT was some time before the children up on the Ferris wheel realized that the machinery was out of order. When they did, they thought at first it was fun to be in the dangling cars, and look over the water and see the twinkling lights of boats coming and going. But presently Marina became frightened.

"I want to go home," she said, stifling a sob.

Nan tried to reassure her by saying the machinery would be fixed at any moment. Nan herself wished she could be sure of this. As she peeked over the side of the car, she could see workmen pulling and pushing at various gadgets. Finally Captain Night came to see what he could do.

A few minutes later the Ferris wheel gave a sudden jerk. The passengers relaxed as it started again. This lasted for only a few seconds, however. Suddenly there was a flash on the ground, and once more the Ferris wheel stopped. Bert and Mateo were now at the top, while Nan and Marina were a few feet below them.

The passengers who were in the cars near the ground climbed out. A few who were not too far up stepped out onto the shoulders of the workmen and were assisted to the ground. But there was no way for those near the top of the wheel to get off.

Marina looked at Nan, tears in her eyes. "Will we have to stay here all night?" she asked, starting to cry.

Nan put her arm around the little girl "Don't be afraid. They will rescue us," she said.

"But how?" Marina sobbed.

"Why—by—with—well, I don't know," Nan confessed.

On the ground there was great excitement. Captain Friday Night had no equipment with which to rescue the stranded passengers. He raced to a telephone and called up the Lakeport Fire Department. He asked them to come at once, bringing the longest ladder they had.

Up in the Ferris wheel the children, of course, did not know what was being planned. A few minutes later they heard the fire whistle blow and presently they could see a hook and ladder racing toward the amusement park.

"Fire!" screamed Marina. "We are going to be burned up!"

Nan had all she could do to hold the little girl in her seat. In her excitement Marina was determined to jump out.

"You *must* sit still," Nan said sternly. Then as a thought came to her, she added, "I know what's going to happen. They're going to rescue us with a ladder."

Presently the hook and ladder turned into the amusement park, but just inside the gate the big fire truck had to stop. There was not much space between the booths. The hook and ladder could not possibly get around in the small area.

Quickly the men unfastened the long extension ladder and hurried to the Ferris wheel with it. The people in the cars nearest the ground were taken down first. The children were last.

Nan, relieved, could smile now.

"It's too bad Freddie had to miss this," she thought. "He would have loved it."

Indeed, Freddie was very envious the next morning when he heard about how the other children had been rescued; how the long ladder had been placed against the Ferris wheel, close to the swinging cars; and how a fireman had climbed up and helped the children down one by one.

"Oh, gee," he said disgustedly, "why do I have to miss everything!"

Bert laughed at his brother. "That's funny, Fred-

die. You know, yesterday when you and Flossie
stayed on the showboat and had supper with the
actors, I wanted to stay but couldn't. So I guess now
things are even."

For several days after this, the twins and the
Castillio children talked about their experiences in
the amusement park and on the showboat. Freddie
and Flossie were invited once more to act with the
midgets. They also had a chance to see the trained
animals and take in some of the other amusements.
Then one evening Captain Night and his company
got ready to leave. The next morning Sam drove the
Bobbsey and the Castillio children down to say good-
bye to them.

"I never had so much fun before in all my life,"
Flossie told the captain, as she shook hands with
him.

He said he wished she and Freddie could join his
company because Mr. M and Mr. X were still unable to act.

"They're pretty old men, and I'm afraid they
won't be able to act much longer, anyway. Now, if
you should ever hear of any midgets who might like
to join my show, please let me know."

"But how will we find you if you're traveling all
around?" Freddie wanted to know.

The captain pulled a card from his pocket. "You
can always reach me through this address," he said,
handing the card to Bert.

The boy doubted that the twins would ever find any midgets for Captain Night, but he thought it would be nice to be able to get in touch with the troupe at some future time. Maybe Dad and Mother would take them on a trip somewhere and they would want to find out if the showboat were near by.

Presently the ship's whistle began to toot. Captain Night ran up the gangplank. The ropes which held the boat were untied, and soon the *Sea Gull* pulled away from the dock.

The children waved to Captain Night and the others on board as long as they could see them. Then they returned to the automobile and climbed in. On the way home all of them looked a little glum.

"It seems as if there isn't anything good to do anymore," Freddie said sadly.

"Oh, I almost forgot," said Mateo. "We are going to have a party for you."

He explained that his mother was going to invite the Bobbsey family to have dinner with them the day after tomorrow.

"Oh, that will be wonderful!" cried Flossie, immediately forgetting to be sad because the showboat had left Lakeport. "Are you—are you going to have Mexican food to eat?" she asked.

Mateo and Marina laughed. It was to be a secret what they would have to eat.

The Bobbsey children could hardly wait for the time to arrive. Promptly at six-thirty on the day of the dinner the twins and their parents presented themselves at the Castillio home. The girls had put on their prettiest dresses, and Bert and Freddie looked very nice in their dark-blue suits.

When Pedro opened the front door, Nan thought she was walking into a lovely garden. Fragrant bouquets of flowers stood everywhere. Mr. and Mrs. Castillio greeted the visitors cordially. After Mr. Bobbsey was introduced, Flossie spoke up:

"Daddy, I'm glad you're meeting the chocolate man at last."

Mr. Bobbsey and Mr. Castillio laughed. Mr. Castillio remarked that this was the first time he had ever been called a chocolate man and he liked the title very much. Mr. Bobbsey asked if everything was coming along well in regard to the candy factory which Mr. Castillio was going to open in Lakeport.

"Yes, thank you," Mr. Castillio replied. "I believe I shall have it running much sooner than I expected."

"Does that mean you won't be staying here so long as you thought?" Nan asked.

"I'm afraid it does, my dear," Mr. Castillio replied.

The Bobbsey twins were sorry to hear this. They had grown very fond of Mateo and Marina, and did not like to think of them leaving so soon.

"Perhaps you will all come to Mexico sometime and visit us," Mrs. Castillio said.

"Oh, that would be nice," cried the twins in unison.

Mr. and Mrs. Bobbsey smiled and said that it would be very pleasant, but at the moment they had no idea of making a trip to Mexico, much as they would like to do so.

"I understand you are in the lumber business, Mr. Bobbsey," Mr. Castillio said. "You should come to my country and see our really fine lumber."

Mr. Bobbsey said that he had often thought of this; in fact, he had had requests for certain kinds of lumber which he could not buy in the United States. Then laughingly he added, "Who knows? One of these days I may decide to accept your kind invitation and visit Mexico."

"And take us with you?" Bert asked eagerly.

"I'll see," was all Mr. Bobbsey would say.

Suddenly Chito began to bark. The guests had thought he was asleep in his basket.

"He's inviting you, too," Marina said, and thanked her pet.

Mr. Bobbsey had not seen the little dog before, and at once made friends with him by stroking his head. At this moment Nan gave a little gasp and rushed across the room to where she had laid the handbag she had brought with her.

"I almost forgot something," she said, opening it. "Here's a picture for you." She handed a photograph to Mrs. Castillio.

"Chito! Oh, what a fine picture of him!" she exclaimed. "Is this the one that was taken the day Chito hid from you at the photographer's?"

"Yes, it is," Nan replied. "He certainly gave us a good scare."

At this moment Pedro appeared at the door. "Dinner is served," he announced.

As the Bobbsey twins followed the older people into the dining room, they wondered what they were going to be served, and whether they would like it.

CHAPTER XI

A MEAN TRICK

SECRETLY Mrs. Bobbsey was a little worried about what they would be given to eat. She did not like her children to eat rich or heavy food, especially in the evening. Moreover, she knew that many Mexican dishes had very spicy sauces. If Freddie or Flossie should get some of this on their tongues, they surely would forget to be polite and would cry out.

The dinner table looked very attractive. Flowers and streamers of green leaves lay along the center, wound in and out among several candlesticks. On a window seat in a basket sat Chito. He was a well-behaved dog, and did not make a sound during the meal. As a reward for his good behavior he was given a biscuit at the end of dinner.

The first course was melon, which the children enjoyed. It was not until a dish of chicken and rice was served that the twins knew a Mexican had prepared the dinner. A sweet-smelling dark sauce was served with it.

Mrs. Castillio suggested that the Bobbsey children put the sauce on the sides of their plates in case they should not like the taste. She asked if her young guests would like to guess what was in it. Smiling, she added:

"I should not expect you to guess everything because the sauce has thirty ingredients. But a few of them, I am sure, you will know."

The twins did much better than she had expected in their guessing. They said corn meal, tomatoes, butter, and Nan even suggested banana, which was right.

Bert did not speak for several minutes. Then he asked slowly:

"Is there chocolate in it?"

Mrs. Castillio's eyes danced. She told the boy he had guessed the secret ingredient, and she thought he was very clever to have detected that taste among so many others.

Flossie then spoke up, making everyone laugh. Looking at Mr. Castillio, she remarked, "You're a chocolate man, so you have to eat lots of chocolate, don't you?" Then she added, "I love chocolate."

"I do, too," said Freddie. "I could eat chocolate candy all day long."

"And become very ill, I'm afraid," said Mrs. Castillio. "My husband does raise cacao trees from which we get chocolate, but we never eat much of it. It's too rich."

Freddie sighed. He said that even so, he believed he would like to live where the cacao trees grow.

"It must smell awfully good," he said, drawing in his breath as if he were imagining the luscious odor. He added that when he grew up he thought he would become a chocolate man himself.

"Freddie's going to be so many things when he grows up!" Nan laughed. "He'll need an airplane to go from one business to another."

She explained that her young brother already had decided to be a fireman, a ship's captain, a detective, a cowboy; and recently he had decided to run a sugar maple farm. The Castillios were amused to hear this, but Mr. Castillio made Freddie feel at ease when he said:

"My son Mateo had similar ideas when he was your age, Freddie. He wanted to carry bananas to market on a mule, he wanted to build a tree house and live with the monkeys, and I seem to recall that he wanted to be a bullfighter also."

"Oh!" cried the Bobbsey twins together, and Nan added fearfully, "Oh, Mateo, that would be an awfully dangerous thing to do. Surely you wouldn't want to be a bullfighter!"

Mateo admitted he had given up the idea, and believed he would stay right at his father's hacienda and run the chocolate business. Moreover, he liked it so well in the United States he hoped the new candy factory would be a great success, and his father would let him come to Lakeport and run it someday. Perhaps Bert would like to become a partner, he added.

"Don't forget me," Freddie said. "I like chocolate better than Bert does. See, I'm eating all my sauce."

Sure enough, Freddie had finished the sauce and eaten everything else on his plate. In fact, the other twins had, too. Mrs. Castillio had seen to it that the meal did not contain any food which her American neighbors might not like. Cups of delicious chocolate were served, and the children learned that this was the same as the drink known to them as cocoa.

When the Bobbseys were ready to leave, Mr. Castillio gave them a box of chocolates which he said had been made on his hacienda, and which he planned to make and sell in Lakeport.

"Freddie," he said, "since you are the chocolate expert," and here a twinkle came into his eye, "suppose you let me know how you like these."

When the twins reached home, Freddie insisted upon opening the box at once. He promised not to eat any of the candy now—as a matter of fact, the little boy had eaten so much dinner he could not swallow another mouthful—but he wanted to see what the chocolates looked like.

"Oh, here's a parrot!" he exclaimed, pointing to a beautifully fashioned bird with a beak and a long tail.

"That's called a cockatoo," his father told him.

In turn, each of the children and their parents pointed out the intriguing-looking candies. They were in the shape of palm trees, monkeys, and other animals, but there was one which the children did not recognize. It looked a little like a turtle, but its shell was in sections, instead of in one piece.

"That's an armadillo," Mrs. Bobbsey told them. As she sent her children off to bed, she said, "There's one kind of armadillo that can roll itself into a hard shiny ball so its enemies can't attack it. I've even heard it can somersault out of danger!"

The next morning when Flossie and Freddie met in the hall they held a whispered conference. Then they hurried down the stairs and spoke to their father, who was just leaving the house.

"Daddy," Flossie said, "Freddie and I want to go see the armadillos."

Mr. Bobbsey said he doubted there were any in the Lakeport zoo. But the twins hastily informed him that they had not meant this. They wanted to go to the land where the armadillos lived.

"So my fat fairy and my little fireman have been scheming together." Mr. Bobbsey grinned. Then he added teasingly, "Suppose you write a letter to the armadillos' hotel and see if they can accommodate us."

With that Mr. Bobbsey opened the door and went

out. The little twins laughed so hard they had to sit down on the floor. Dinah found them there and, pulling them to their feet, led them to the breakfast table. Before they could eat they had to tell her all about the dinner at the Castillio home, and show her the unusual pieces of chocolate candy.

"Yo' all bettah let me take charge ob dis heah candy!" Dinah said. "When yo' want a piece to eat, jes come an' ask me."

"But I won't just say candy," Flossie told the cook. "I'll come and say, 'Dinah, may I have a monkey to eat this morning?' "

"And I'll say," Freddie put in, " 'Dinah, I want a whole palm tree today.' "

Dinah chuckled as she took the box of candy to the kitchen and brought back some orange juice for them. Presently Nan and Bert came downstairs and the younger children asked them what they were going to do. Bert said he, Charlie Mason, and Mateo were going down to the place where the traveling amusement park had been. Maybe they could find some souvenirs that had been left behind. Nan had a date with Nellie Parks to shop for a birthday present for Mrs. Parks.

"I'm going over to play with Marina," Flossie announced.

Freddie said nothing, but he suddenly felt very much alone. He decided to find Teddy Blake and get him to play a boys' game. After the others had left, the little Bobbsey boy sat thinking what boys' game there was that girls did not play.

"Girls play most everything boys do," he told himself. "Baseball, football——" Then an idea came to him. He recalled seeing a junk pile in a lot not far from where Captain Night's show had been. "I'll make believe I'm driving that truck down there and Teddy can be a policeman directing the traffic."

Now, unfortunately, it happened that sometimes when Freddie got an idea, he forgot to tell anyone at home about it. This happened to be one of those times. He hurried from the house, going at once to Teddy Blake's.

"Hi, Ted!" he called to his playmate, who was sitting on the front steps of his home. "I've got a swell idea for a game."

Quickly he told his friend about the junk yard where old, battered automobiles were piled up. But the truck, which stood off by itself, was not in too bad condition to be used for a game. Teddy's eyes sparkled. He was thrilled with the idea of playing policeman while Freddie was the truck driver.

Teddy also forgot to tell his family where he was going, so as they ran down the street, no one knew where they were heading. But there was one person who suddenly became very interested in what they were doing. Danny Rugg, on his way to the Bobbsey house to pick a fight with Bert, saw the two little fellows hurrying off.

"Freddie will do just as well," the bully said to himself. "Those Bobbseys got me into a mess, and I'm going to get square!"

Turning on his heel, he followed Freddie and his friend. Danny was surprised when the lads stopped at the wire-enclosed junk yard. The gate was locked, and no one was around.

The fence was not very high. At once Freddie Bobbsey decided that he and Teddy could climb the fence. In a jiffy they were over it, and walking toward the truck, which was on the far side of the lot.

Quickly Danny jumped the fence and hastened after them. He hid behind a broken-down roadster and watched Freddie climb aboard the truck and take his place behind the wheel. Teddy pulled a whistle from his pocket, held up his hand, and blew hard. Freddie jammed on the brakes just the way he had seen Daddy do it in their car. Presently Teddy insisted upon changing places, and the game went on for a few more minutes.

Danny wondered what he might do to get Freddie in a fix. Suddenly an idea came to him. Moving away quietly, he crawled underneath a pile of the junk. Then he started to meow like a cat in trouble.

"What's that?" Freddie asked suddenly, hearing he sounds.

"A cat, of course," replied Teddy, not much interested.

"But it sounds as if it's hurt," the Bobbsey boy insisted.

"I guess you're right," Teddy agreed.

He climbed down from the truck, and the two little boys began searching for the injured cat. It was not hard to trace the sound, and soon they came to the cavelike pile of junk. It was dark inside, and Freddie could not see Danny hiding there.

"I'll go in there and get the cat," Freddie offered.

Getting down on his hands and knees, he crawled inside. Suddenly, before he knew what was happening, a figure pushed past him. An instant later Teddy was grabbed by the shoulders and pushed into the hole after Freddie.

Danny quickly pulled part of a wrecked car from the top of the pile and wedged it tightly in the entrance of the hole. Then, with a laugh, he ran off, jumped the fence, and left his two prisoners.

CHAPTER XII

THE MISSING BOYS

"WHERE'S Freddie?" Mrs. Bobbsey asked Dinah before lunchtime.

"I don't rightly know, Mis' Bobbsey," the cook replied. "I thought he was playin' wif Flossie."

"Freddie wasn't playing with Marina and me," Flossie said. "I haven't seen Freddie all morning."

They decided he must have gone with Bert or Nan, but when the older twins came in, they reported that Freddie had not been with them. At this point Mrs. Bobbsey became somewhat alarmed. She went to the telephone and called the homes of several of his friends. Freddie was not at any of their houses, but Mrs. Blake reported that Teddy also was missing.

"It's possible the two boys are together," she said, "but I have no idea where they went."

Bert and Nan offered to search for them. They went from place to place, asking at various houses if anyone had seen the boys. No one had.

Lunchtime came and went. The afternoon wore

on. Still the two small boys did not appear. By five o'clock Mr. Bobbsey, who had been notified, decided to get in touch with the police. At once a general alarm was sent out by radio.

Now it happened that Danny Rugg had turned on a small radio in his bedroom. All of a sudden he heard the startling announcement that Freddie Bobbsey and Teddy Blake were missing. Danny began to shake with fright. He had not expected that the trick he had played on the two little boys would have any serious results. The mean boy had figured it would take the two boys only a little while to push the junk out of the way and free themselves. Suddenly he realized that probably they still were prisoners. Then an even worse thought occurred to Danny. What if the pile of junk had fallen on Freddie and Ted!

Danny did not know what to do. The boy was afraid to tell his mother. Finally he decided, while she was in the kitchen with the door closed, to use the telephone in the front hall. Dialing the Bobbsey house, he waited for someone to say hello. When Mrs. Bobbsey answered, he said in as deep a voice as he could:

"Go look in the junk yard!"

"What did you say?" Mrs. Bobbsey asked, startled at the words. But the person at the other end of the line had hung up.

Danny went back to his room to listen to the radio

for an announcement that the two boys had been safely rescued. In the meantime, Mrs. Bobbsey called police headquarters and asked the captain if there were a junk pile in town. Hearing that there was one, she told the officer about the mysterious message.

At once two policemen set off for the junk yard. One policeman searched the left side of the yard and the other policeman took the right-hand side. Then one of them called out:

"Freddie! Teddy! Teddy! Freddie!"

Inside their little prison the two boys lay sound asleep. Having shouted themselves hoarse for a couple of hours, they could no longer call for help. Exhausted, they had gone to sleep.

The policemen continued their search all over the place, but they could see no one. Finally they decided the missing boys were not there. They were just about to go away, when Freddie wakened and thought he heard voices. A moment later he was sure he did.

"Help! Help!" he cried.

Although his voice was hoarse, it still could be heard. At the gate of the junk yard the two policemen stood still. Had they heard a cry for help, or had they just imagined it? Standing very quiet, they listened attentively.

"Help! Help!" they heard.

By this time Teddy, too, was awake, and added his voice to Freddie's cries. A moment later the policemen traced the sounds. They pulled away the battered piece of junk from the doorway of the cave. Freddie and his friend crawled out.

The policemen picked up the two little boys and carried them to the gate. There they were transferred to the arms of Mr. Bobbsey and Mr. Blake, who had followed the patrolmen.

Mrs. Bobbsey and Mrs. Blake were there also. Tears of happiness rolled down their cheeks at the safe return of their small sons. The two boys sobbed out their story, and promised never again to go away from home without telling their parents where they would be.

"But who shut you in there?" Mr. Bobbsey demanded grimly.

"A big boy," Freddie replied. "I don't know who he was."

When Nan and Bert heard the story a little later, they, too, wondered who would play such a mean trick. Bert instantly felt sure it must be Danny Rugg. When his mother said that just because Danny played horrid tricks at times, he should not be accused unjustly at this time, Bert said:

"Just the same, I'll bet he was trying to get square with us for finding him out about what he did on the showboat."

The Bobbsey twin wanted to set out at once to prove his idea, but his parents insisted he should not leave the house again that evening. Furthermore, they reminded him that it was always good to sleep over any idea hatched in anger. The following morning Bert was of the same opinion, however. He confided his thought to Nan, adding:

"But I don't know how to prove it."

His sister suggested that they might follow the same method they had used on the showboat to pick up a clue. The two children went to the junk yard, climbed the fence, and began their search.

They had no sooner begun when two strange boys jumped the fence to help. Five minutes later two more came. Then a boy and a girl arrived. Within half an hour a dozen children were combing the junk yard, all with the same idea Bert had had; that the boy who had trapped Freddie and Teddy should be punished. No one but Bert, however, suspected Danny Rugg.

There was such confusion in the lot that no one could be sure that anything he picked up was a clue. Suddenly the owner of the junk yard arrived. At once he ordered all the children out of the place. Bert stopped a moment to explain that he was Freddie's brother, and why he was there.

"Then I don't blame you," said the man. "Come, I'll go in with you."

He and the Bobbsey twins started a search for clues all over again, but they found nothing. Meanwhile, Danny Rugg lived in panic for several days. Although he knew Freddie and Teddy had been found unharmed he was fearful of being found out. When days went by, however, and no one accused him, he felt much better.

During those same days nothing so exciting as Freddie's adventure happened to the twins. They played with Mateo and Marina, and learned more and more about customs and people in Mexico.

Nan had a little secret which she was not telling anyone. For an hour each day she was privately taking lessons in Spanish from Anita. The kindly Indian woman was very patient with her young pupil. At first Nan felt as if she never could remember the words. But each time she was alone she would practice them, and after a week she surprised Anita by all she had learned.

Now Nan had intended keeping the secret to herself for a while, but one day after the Castillios had been in Lakeport for almost a month, her mother overheard her actually talking to herself in Spanish!

"Why, Nan," she cried, coming into the girl's room. "This is wonderful, dear. Have the Castillios been teaching you how to speak their language?"

Nan smiled. *"Si,* Señora," she replied. *"Quiere usted estudiar Español?"*

Mrs. Bobbsey laughed. She was very pleased indeed, and gave her daughter a tight hug. Nan begged her to keep the secret.

"But why are you learning Spanish?" Mrs. Bobbsey asked.

"Just in case we go to Mexico," Nan answered, pronouncing Mexico in the Spanish way.

"You must have overheard Daddy talking, Nan," her mother declared.

"No, I didn't," Nan said, puzzled. Then she asked eagerly, "Have *I* found out a secret? Is Daddy going down to Mexico to look at trees? Is he going to take us all with him?"

Mrs. Bobbsey said she could not answer that, but the fact that she did not say no excited Nan. She raced off to tell Bert. He in turn said "Hooray!" so loudly that Flossie and Freddie wanted to know what it was all about. Nan told them, but warned them that perhaps nothing would come of it.

The small twins could not keep such important news a secret. They asked their mother's permission to walk down to Mr. Bobbsey's office and drive home with him that evening. When she gave her consent, they hurried away as fast as they could. Bursting in upon their father at the lumber office, they cried out together:

"When are we going?"

"Going where?" Mr. Bobbsey asked.

The next second he was laughing loudly, because Flossie was wagging her finger at him just the way she had seen Dinah wag hers at Sam.

"Daddy, it's no use trying to keep it a secret any longer. When are we going to Mexico?" she asked him.

Mr. Bobbsey hardly knew what to say. As a matter of fact, he had recently decided to go to Mexico and take his family with him, but he had not wanted to tell them until he was sure of his plans. Seeing the two eager faces looking at him, he put one arm around Flossie, the other around Freddie, and said:

"We might go as soon as next week!"

CHAPTER XIII

THE CANDY FACTORY

HEARING a great commotion in his office, Mr. Bobbsey's secretary rushed in. She was sure something had happened, because she had heard a squeal, a scream, and then thumping sounds.

As she hurried in, Miss Munson saw only a small but happy family group. Mr. Bobbsey's younger twins were crying out in delight and jumping up and down.

"We're going to Mexico! We're going to Mexico!" Flossie told Miss Munson excitedly. "Only you pronounce it May-hee-koh."

Miss Munson looked at Mr. Bobbsey, who grinned sheepishly.

"My children have found me out!" he said.

"You mean they know everything?" his secretary asked.

The twins' father said indeed they did not. All they knew was that he *might* go to Mexico and take his family with him. But what part of Mexico they would visit and what they would see, he was not telling. Freddie and Flossie pleaded with him to tell them more, but he refused.

A few minutes later he put away the papers on his desk and took the children home in his car. All that evening the Bobbsey household buzzed with conversation about the proposed trip. Flossie had a long talk with Dinah on what clothes to take.

"Goodness sakes, chile," said the kindly old cook. "Some places in Mexico is very cool; others is very hot. Ef yo' don' know what town yo' all is gwine to, how in de world would I know what clothes yo' ought to take?"

The next morning Flossie and Nan looked over everything in their closet, as well as in their bureau drawers. They spent nearly an hour trying to figure out which clothes they would need, but in the end they put everything away, and decided to ask the Castillios about it.

The two girls hurried across the street. No one was at home but Pedro and Anita. It looked very much as if they were packing some of the things the family had brought with them.

"Are you going home?" Flossie asked.

She learned that Mr. Castillio had finished his business in Lakeport. He was now trying to get plane reservations for them all to return to Mexico.

"Mrs. Castillio is downtown now with the children, buying them some clothes," Anita said. "We do not live near any stores. About twice a year Mr.

and Mrs. Castillio go to the city and buy what we need."

"Is it hot or cold where you live?" Flossie asked.

"Oh, it is very warm all the time where we live," Anita said. "Cacao trees only grow where it is warm."

Nan wanted to ask whether Anita knew if the Bobbseys were going to visit the Castillios' hacienda, but she was too polite to do this. Once, when she thought Flossie was going to, she shook her head at her little sister.

For the next hour Flossie played with Chito, and Nan took her Spanish lesson. Flossie, hearing her sister speaking the strange words, was very proud of her. She decided to learn Spanish herself someday.

Presently the telephone rang. Mr. Castillio was calling to ask Pedro to bring Nan and Flossie down to the chocolate factory. Bert and Freddie already were there, and he thought the girls might enjoy seeing the place too. Pedro called a taxi, and they drove at once to the new building on the outskirts of Lakeport.

Flossie was a little disappointed as she went inside. The little girl expected the place to smell sweet with the aroma of chocolate candy. There was only the odor of fresh paint. But she walked around quietly with the other children as Mr. Castillio explained his modern method of making candy.

"No hands touch a single piece of it," he said. "First we boil the syrup in these big vats." He pointed to two enormous copper vats.

"They're big enough to cook a giant's dinner in, aren't they?" Freddie remarked. "Maybe a whole lot of giants," he added.

This made the little boy think of the giant who had rescued him from the merry-go-round. It also reminded him of the midgets, and he wondered how Mr. M and Mr. X were getting along. A moment later he spoke his thoughts aloud.

"Oh, I saw an item about the showboat in a Hillsboro paper," Mr. Castillio said. Hillsboro was a town a couple of hundred miles from Lakeport. "It gave the program, but did not mention the midgets, so I presume they did not give their play."

The Bobbseys were sure that was because the two little men who had been injured were not well enough to act.

"We must find some midgets for the showboat," Flossie spoke up. "You remember, Captain Night asked us to."

She and Freddie stayed behind the others to talk about the little men, when suddenly they heard the whirr of machinery. The twins hurried off to look at the candy-making apparatus. It had two enormous arms which went up and down very fast.

Mr. Castillio explained that these arms would

make chocolate taffy. He turned off the machine and walked into the next room. Freddie and Flossie again hung behind. Freddie had an idea he would like to turn the switch as he had seen Mr. Castillio do. But Flossie stopped her brother just in time.

"You mustn't touch anything," she warned him.

Freddie might not have obeyed, but at this moment he spied two large barrels in the corner of the room. At once he went over to see what was in them. Flossie followed. One barrel was tightly closed, but the lid of the other came off easily. The barrel was as high as Freddie and Flossie, however, and they could not see over the edge of it.

The little twins grabbed the rim tightly with their hands and jumped up to look inside. The barrel was only half filled, and the children's tug was too much for it. Over it came!

The twins were knocked to the floor. The barrel fell on top of them, showering its contents over the boy and girl.

"Woof!" Freddie said, half smothered.

His little sister could not speak at all. The brown, dusty powder which had fallen on them was powdered chocolate, and her mouth was full of it.

At this moment Nan missed her small brother and sister. Leaving the others, she came back to hunt for them. What a sight met her eyes!

Freddie and Flossie looked just like two big chocolate dolls. They were just rising from the heap of brown powder on the floor. The mishap had not hurt either of them, but they made a truly strange picture. Both children had brown hair in place of their golden curls, and their light clothing was chocolate-covered.

"Oh, Nan!" cried Flossie. "Please do something. I'm g-g-going—"

With that, the little girl began to sneeze and could not stop. A moment later Freddie began. Nan did not know what to do. Mr. Castillio came into the room. When he saw the younger twins, he guessed at once what had happened, and led them to a spot in the wall where there was an outlet for a suction cleaner. He lifted up the cap and told them to put their heads near it. In a few moments most of the brown powder had been sucked away, and the two children looked more like themselves.

They apologized for having upset the barrel of chocolate, and then Nan said they would have to go home so the children could have baths and shampoos.

"Maybe when you put water on me, I'll be chocolate candy," Flossie remarked.

Mr. Castillio laughed. "Not unless we put sugar with you and boil you for a while," he said.

The chocolate had a bitter taste, and Freddie and Flossie were glad to have nice cold drinks of water before leaving the factory. Bert stayed a moment to tell Mr. Castillio and Mateo that the Bobbsey family might be going to Mexico.

"Yes, I know," said Mr. Castillio. "Your father and I have been discussing the possibility of his getting lumber down there."

Bert grinned. "Dad didn't say what part of Mexico he was going to, but the trees he might buy are down near your hacienda, aren't they?"

"Yes, they are in that area," Mr. Castillio said, his eyes twinkling. "My invitation to the Bobbsey family still holds."

On reaching home Bert told his twin what he had learned. "Do you suppose we're going to Mexico with the Castillios?" he asked her.

Nan wondered also. Various happenings of the past few days seemed to point that way. Something else happened too, which seemed to confirm this. On one of her visits to the Castillio home, Nan overheard Pedro speak to Anita in Spanish.

She did not mean to listen, but Pedro spoke so loudly she could not help hearing what he said, and she could understand every word.

Excitedly she dashed back to the Bobbsey house to tell Bert only to learn that he had gone to find Danny Rugg.

"He said sumpin' 'bout a clue," Dinah told her. "He said dat mean boy was goin' to get his."

Dinah had noticed that Bert was angry about something, and she had advised him to watch his step.

"Mebbe yo' bettah go find him, Nan," she suggested, "befo' he gits hisself in trouble."

Nan wondered if Bert had found out something that had to do with Freddie's experience in the junk yard. She knew Bert suspected Danny of being the boy who had made prisoners of Freddie and Ted Blake.

Following Dinah's advice, Nan set off for Danny Rugg's house. On reaching it, she looked in the back yard. Finding no one there, she rang the bell. Nobody came to open the door, so Nan concluded the family must be out.

"Where in the world did Bert go?" his twin asked herself.

She did not know where to look for him. Finally Nan decided to go to the junk yard. When she came to the fence which surrounded it, she heard cries and shouts from inside.

The next moment her brother and the bully came into sight. Both were lashing out with their fists!

CHAPTER XIV

FUN AT THE PARTY

NAN stood horrified for a second. Then she cried out to the boys to stop fighting. Whether they did not hear her, or whether they simply would not pay attention, she did not know. But the fight went on.

Quickly Nan climbed the fence. She did not blame her brother for wanting to fight Danny, but she was fearful one of her brother's teeth might be knocked out, because the other boy seemed to be trying to hit Bert in the mouth.

"Stop!" she cried, racing up to them. "Stop!"

Actually she did not expect the two boys to stop fighting. Great was her surprise when Danny suddenly dodged a blow from Bert, and took to his heels. Quickly climbing the fence, he raced off up the road.

For a few seconds Bert stood puffing. Then he laughed. "Why, Nan, Danny was afraid of you."

"Afraid of me?" Nan asked, not understanding what he meant.

"I guess he thought you were going to fight him, too," Bert said. "With both of us, he couldn't take it."

Nan laughed too. Fighting with Danny Rugg was furthest from her thoughts. Nevertheless, she was glad she had scared the bully away. She asked Bert what had happened.

"I met Charlie Mason," her twin explained. "He overheard Danny telling someone he had cooped up a couple of fellows in a junk pile. I was sure he meant Freddie and Ted, so I went after Danny. When he saw me coming, he ran, and for a long time I couldn't find him. But I thought maybe he'd hide down here."

"And he owned up?" Nan asked.

"I made him. He said he didn't see why everybody made such a fuss over it, because Freddie and Ted weren't hurt. But I told him he had no right to scare us all the way he did, and then he started the fight."

Nan was glad the battle between the two boys was over. As the twins walked home, she told her brother the latest news about their coming trip to Mexico, and how she suspected they might be going with the Castillios.

"I heard Pedro telling Anita they were going on ahead to get the house on the hacienda ready for the visitors," Nan stated.

Anita had said the Bobbseys would stop off to see

some of the interesting sights before coming to the hacienda. Nan presumed they meant the pyramids, and some of the Indian villages. Suddenly she said, "Oh!"

"What's the matter?" asked Bert.

"We ought to have a party for Mateo and Marina before they leave Lakeport," his twin announced. "They've met most of our friends, but we haven't had a party."

Bert liked parties. There was always something specially good to eat at them, and prizes for games. But he did not like planning for them as well as Nan did.

"You fix it up," Bert told his sister.

When they reached home, Nan hurried upstairs to ask her mother if they might give a party. Mrs. Bobbsey thought this would be a nice thing to do. Her daughter wanted to know if it would be polite to ask Marina and Mateo to play for the other guests.

"Marina can play the piano, and Mateo plays the guitar. He didn't bring a guitar with him, but we could rent one from the music store, couldn't we?" Nan asked her mother.

"I believe so," said Mrs. Bobbsey. "What else would you like to do at the party?"

Nan wanted to do something unusual; something which the Mexican children had never done. She and her mother talked for a long while, trying to decide. At last they decided, and then Nan made out her list of guests.

First the Castillio children were invited, and then several friends of Nan, Bert, Flossie, and Freddie. The party was held two days later.

When the guests arrived, they found what they thought were peanut plants set here and there in the hall and the living room. Actually they were not peanut plants at all. They were green plants Mrs. Bobbsey had ordered from the florist, and the twins had hung peanuts on them. Mrs. Bobbsey asked Flossie and Freddie's friends to guess what was the matter with the "peanut" plants.

"I think peanuts grow upside down," Susie Larker remarked, "and these hang down."

Mrs. Bobbsey said that was not correct, and that Susie must be thinking of bananas. Next Ted Blake took a guess, saying only one peanut grew on a stem; not several. But he was wrong too.

None of the small children in the room seemed to know, but Mrs. Bobbsey noticed that Marina's eyes were sparkling mischievously and asked her if she knew what was the matter with the peanut plants.

"I believe peanuts grow under the ground like potatoes," Marina answered.

This was the correct answer, and the small Lakeport children felt embarrassed that they had not known this. Marina had never seen peanuts growing, but she said that she had learned about them from her tutor.

Presently the peanuts were taken from the plants and laid in several rows on the floor. Then the older children had a peanut relay race, with the boys against the girls. The first boy had to pick up each peanut on a spoon and carry it to a bowl. The next boy had to take them out and lay them on the floor again. The third had to pick them up, and so on.

The girls were doing the same thing across the room. As the game got near the end, Nellie Parks and Mateo were the two left in it. Both were so excited that each dropped the last peanut off the spoon three times and had to pick it up. The game ended in a tie.

The small children took their turn at the game, but they had more trouble. The peanuts kept falling from the spoons and rolling under the furniture. In trying to pick them up again, the youngsters would get in one another's way. In colliding they would knock more peanuts to the floor. At one point in the game all the children were on their hands and knees reaching under tables and chairs for peanuts so the game could go on.

In the meantime Waggo, shut in the cellar, had managed to push open the door, and now he came bounding into the room. The little fox terrier was supposed to have stayed in the cellar because Mrs.

Bobbsey knew that if he came to the party something would be bound to happen.

And something did happen! Waggo squeezed himself first under one chair, then another, grabbed the peanuts in his mouth, and crushed them. In backing out from under the sofa he got between the feet of Flossie's friend Mary Wenton, upsetting the little girl. Down she went with a hard thump, and tears came into her eyes.

"Waggo Bobbsey, you can't stay at this party!" Flossie said severely.

Grabbing the little dog up in her arms, she put him back in the cellar. But this did not please Waggo at all. He began to bark and to scratch on the door. Dinah finally let him out and tied him in the back yard. Waggo did not like this any better than being in the cellar. He barked even louder.

Suddenly Bert decided that it might be fun to let Waggo entertain his friends. Recently he had taught the little dog, who had once performed in a circus, some new tricks. Also, he had bought him a little costume.

Quietly Bert left the room, got his pet, and took him to his bedroom. First, he strapped stilts to the dog's hind legs. Then he dressed him in a suit like those which monkeys wear when they accompany organ grinders. A little red hat, perched on top of Waggo's head, was held in place by a strap under his chin. A long, brown monkey tail fitted snugly in place over Waggo's own tail. Bert picked up the dog in his arms, fitted the handle of a little tin cup over one paw, and said:

"Now, funny-face, do your tricks!"

Bert took a music box from his chiffonier. As he walked down the stairs he started the music playing.

When the boy walked into the living room, the guests began to laugh. They knew the animal in Bert's arms, with the long hind legs and long, waving tail was really Waggo, but they were eager to see how much like a monkey he could act.

Waggo loved to do tricks, and he was well trained. Stalking around the room, he held out the paw with the little cup. Bert kept the music going. The children began dropping various things into the cup. A few of them had pennies with them, but those who had no money dropped in rings, bracelets, hair clips, and anything else they could think of, knowing they would get them back later.

Of all the children, none were so amused as Mateo and Marina. Their own little dog Chito could do no tricks at all, and they thought Waggo was wonderful. Marina even whispered to Flossie that she thought it would be nice if the Bobbseys would take Waggo to Mexico with them.

"We could have a little show at the hacienda," Marina said.

Flossie, too, thought this would be a wonderful idea. She decided to ask her father about it when he came home.

After Waggo had finished his little act, Mrs. Bobbsey suggested that the children play "I'm Going to Mexico." The smaller children were grouped in one circle, the older ones in another. The twins' mother explained that each child was to name something to put in a suitcase, and also to repeat all the articles which had been mentioned before it was his turn to speak.

As she stood listening to the two groups, she smiled broadly. The articles which the children mentioned were far too large to go in a suitcase, and not at all practical to use on such a long trip. She heard Teddy call out "Express Wagon." Susie said she would take along a piano. Of all the children, only Mateo was able to mention all the articles named in his group. Mrs. Bobbsey handed him a prize, saying:

"When *you* go to Mexico, I hope you will be able to use this."

The boy unwrapped the little package and found a deck of cards. But they were not regular playing cards. With them the boy would be able to do tricks. He would be able to find any card which someone in his audience might pick out, no matter how much he shuffled them. And also he would be able to make a particular card pop right out of the pack!

The Mexican boy was thrilled with his prize. He had never seen a pack of trick cards and knew he would have lots of fun with them at the hacienda.

After eating Dinah's delicious ice cream and cake the children left, saying they had had a wonderful time, and that if the Bobbseys should go to Mexico, they hoped the twins would have a wonderful time there, too.

Just as the last guest went out the door, Mr. Bobbsey turned into the driveway. He parked the car instead of putting it into the garage.

"Oh, something important's going to happen!" cried Nan.

The twins had noticed that whenever their father had anything special on his mind, he never put the car in the garage when he came home. If he had an important announcement to make, he always left the car standing in the driveway.

The twins waited eagerly to hear what their father was going to say this time.

CHAPTER XV

"YES, I have the tickets," Mr. Bobbsey announced, as the four eager twins crowded around him.

Flossie tried to climb up to hug him. And Freddie, in his enthusiasm to do a somersault, almost knocked his father over.

"When does the train go?" Nan asked excitedly.

Mr. Bobbsey said they were not going by train. Bert remarked it would be a pretty long drive for his father, but supposed his mother would help with the driving.

Mr. Bobbsey grinned. "Come in here and I'll show you something," he directed.

They followed him into the living room. From his pocket he drew out six pieces of paper. He handed one to Bert, one to Nan, and suggested they read them.

Bert gave a whoop. "Gee whiz!" he cried out. "We're going by plane! We're going all the way to Mexico by plane!"

119

The Bobbsey twins had been in airplanes several times, but this would be the longest ride they had ever had at one time. Mr. Bobbsey had brought several maps and folders of pictures, showing the various places at which the plane would stop.

"What part of Mexico are we going to?" Nan asked.

Her father explained that they were going to what we call Mexico City, but down in Mexico it is called Mexico, D. F. They would stay at a hotel there for a little while and do some sight-seeing.

"After that we'll go on south," Mr. Bobbsey told them.

When he did not say where, and the children had waited several seconds for him to tell them, Flossie finally blurted out:

"Are we going to the Castillios' ha—ha—hacienda?" Flossie had at last learned the word and did not have to be helped in pronouncing it.

"That's right, my fat fairy," her father replied. "The Castillios will leave Lakeport with us and fly straight home. They're not going to stop off in Mexico City."

The small twins reminded him that he had not yet told them when they were leaving. He smiled, and agreed that certainly was an important item. They would leave one week from that day and would stop in New York City a few hours so he could attend to some business there.

What a hubbub the Bobbsey household was in during the next week! It would be hard to say who the busiest person was, but it seemed to Nan that Dinah was everywhere at once; in the laundry, in the kitchen, and on the second floor, each time coming and going with freshly laundered clothes. Somehow the kindly cook also managed to prepare tasty meals and keep the house in order.

But sometimes the poor woman's patience was tried to the breaking point. Several times she had to insist that Freddie and Flossie put away toys which they hoped to carry to Mexico. At one point Flossie actually had six dolls lined up on her bed ready to take on the trip!

"Don't yo' know dey's mo' dolls in Mexico dan in dis country?" Dinah said. "Dey have whole markets full o' dolls. Yo' bettah bring some home, Flossie, 'stead o' takin' some down."

Freddie knew he would not be permitted to take any of his fire engines except maybe the very smallest one. But he did get hold of all the straw hats in the house which his father wore. Dinah found him busy one morning stuffing paper inside the crowns, trying to make them small enough to fit his own head.

"What in de world is yo' tryin' to do?" the cook asked him.

Freddie explained that it was so hot where they were going in the south of Mexico that he would need a big straw hat. So he would just have to borrow one of Daddy's.

Dinah laughed. "Don't yo' know dey makes millions of hats in Mexico? Big ones and little ones. Yo' can buy jes de right size to fit yo'."

Freddie finally put away the hats. He and Flossie decided to go outdoors and play. At first they could think of no game. Then suddenly Freddie had an idea. He told it to his twin. Flossie giggled enthusiastically, then the two of them ran off down the street.

"The hay is in here," Freddie remarked a few minutes later, turning into the driveway of an empty house. "It's in the barn back there," he added, pointing.

The children ran to the barn, and from the floor gathered up large armfuls of the dry hay. They took so much of it that they could not see ahead of them as they walked back up the street.

On reaching their own house again, the small twins began building a little house. First they got four pickets from an old fence which had been torn down. One by one they hammered these into the ground at the side of the garage. Next they got newspapers and stretched these between the posts. As soon as one side wall of the little house was ready, Flossie draped the hay over it. In a little while three walls were up.

"It has to have a roof, Freddie," his twin announced. "How are you going to put that on?"

Freddie was not sure, but he found that newspapers would reach across. He tacked them in place and then the children heaped hay on top. They walked off a little distance to look at their work. Freddie was pretty proud of it.

"It looks just like some Mexican Indian huts I saw in the picture," he declared. "Only this one's much littler."

"What are you going to do with it?" Flossie wanted to know.

Freddie would not tell her, even though she said he was mean not to, after she had helped him build it. As a matter of fact, Freddie had something startling in mind, but he did not want to mention it yet.

In disgust, Flossie walked off. She decided to go across the street and find Marina. This suited Freddie very well. It would give him time to figure out what he wanted to have happen without disobeying his mother.

"Mother said I must never touch matches," he told himself. "But I wish the Mexican hut would get on fire so I could put it out."

While he was thinking about this, Freddie went to get out his biggest fire engine. Dragging it from the garage, he filled the tank with water, and pulled it a little distance off from his Mexican hut.

The small boy sat down on the back steps of the house and stared straight ahead of him. Then suddenly he could hardly believe what he saw. There was smoke curling up from the back of his newly made hut! Two seconds later the whole thing burst into flames. This was more than Freddie had hoped for!

He was almost too startled to remember what he had planned to do. He screamed loudly for Dinah, then dashed toward his fire engine. Dinah was in the cellar at the time and it took her several seconds to get upstairs and outside. By this time Freddie was playing his fire hose on the burning hay.

Dinah, surprised, and worried for fear the garage might catch fire, dashed forward to help, but there was no need. Freddie's big fire engine held enough water to put out the blaze, and he had practiced so many times with it that he now knew exactly what to do.

The fire was soon out and Dinah started to scold Freddie. It was several minutes before she became convinced that he had not set the fire. He admitted having wanted the hay hut to burn up, but it had seemed to set itself on fire.

"Dat couldn't happen," Dinah declared. "If yo' didn't do it, den somebody else did."

When the rest of the family heard what had happened, Bert rushed to the back of their property to look for footprints of the person who probably had set the fire. He had no trouble finding them in the soft earth.

"I'll bet some boy was here," he declared.

His mother said this did not prove the hut had been set on fire by that boy. The footprints could have been made before Freddie and Flossie got the hay.

But Bert was sure the prints would prove who had set the hut afire. There was no time for him to do any detective work, however. Going to the telephone, he called up his friend Charlie Mason and asked him to come over. Bert pointed out the footprints and asked Charlie if he would try to find out, while the Bobbseys were in Mexico, who had caused the fire.

"I sure will," Charlie promised.

The boy got two pieces of white paper. He laid one over the footprint made by the boy's right foot, and the other over the left. Then with a knife he carefully cut around the edges. As he held up the two pieces, shaped like shoes, Nan remarked laughingly:

"It'll be like going out to find Cinderella. Only

you have a paper shoe instead of a glass slipper."

Charlie did not feel as if he were going after any Cinderella. He was sure he was going to find some mean boy.

"If you catch him before we get home," said Bert, "will you write and tell me?"

"You bet I will," Charlie agreed.

That afternoon the Bobbseys did their final packing. Since they were limited in the number of pounds of baggage each one might take on the plane, they kept running back and forth to the bathroom scale to weigh the suitcases. Extra shoes were removed. A traveling clock was taken out and several bottles were set back on Mrs. Bobbsey's bureau. At last the baggage was just the correct number of pounds.

Across the street the Castillios were having the same trouble. They had bought many things while in Lakeport. Finally they gave up trying to take everything by plane and came to the Bobbsey house for help in shipping the articles to Mexico. There was always lumber in the cellar of the Bobbsey home, and Sam worked until midnight constructing boxes in which to pack the articles. He promised to send the boxes off the following day.

The next morning the Castillios came over to breakfast, since Pedro and Anita already had left. Dinah had prepared an especially fine meal, and Mr. Castillio remarked, with a twinkle in his eye, that if

Dinah should ever get tired of cooking in the United States, she would be welcome to come and take charge of his hacienda.

"Yo' couldn't get mah feet off dis here United States soil." She grinned. "It's all right for de family to go visitin', but dey's got to be sure to come back to ole Sam and Dinah."

The Bobbsey twins quickly assured the faithful cook that they certainly would come back. Nevertheless, they could hardly wait to be off on their trip. There were so many things to be seen, and Flossie, especially, felt she had a particular piece of work to do in Mexico. Captain Friday Night needed some new little men for his show. While she was in Mexico, Flossie was going to try very hard to find some duendes for him.

"Everybody ready?" called Mr. Bobbsey from the front hall a couple of hours later. "We'd better be on our way."

The Bobbsey car could not hold all the travelers, so a taxicab had been called. It already was standing at the door and the Castillios' suitcases were being piled into it.

The children put on their coats and hats, said good-bye to Dinah, and climbed into the car. Sam pulled away from the curb and headed for the airport. The taxicab followed with the four Castillios. When the Bobbseys reached the airport, each of them in turn got on a scale to be weighed. Then their tickets were stamped and they were directed to a room to wait for the plane. Presently a voice over the loud-speaker called out that the plane they were to take was coming in.

"But, Dad," Nan said, suddenly grasping her father's arm, "the Castillios aren't here yet!"

Mr. Bobbsey, who had assumed the others were right back of them, became alarmed. He dashed to the other room, the twins following close on his heels. They looked all over the place. Mateo and Marina and their parents were not in sight.

"Oh, what has happened to them?" Nan cried fearfully.

CHAPTER XVI

ALL ABOARD

MR. BOBBSEY hurried outside the building and looked up and down. There was no taxi in sight. He felt helpless. It would be dreadful if the Castillios missed the plane. But if he were to go and hunt for them, then the Bobbseys, too, would miss the plane.

"If I had only kept Sam!" he exclaimed. "He might have gone to find them. The taxi must have broken down."

As a matter of fact, Sam at this very moment was rescuing the Castillio family. He had waited at the airport, planning to watch the Bobbseys take off, but noticing that the taxi had not driven up and that the time was getting short, he had gone to the car and hurried down the road.

The airport was several miles out of Lakeport, and Sam knew that if the taxicab had broken down there might be no one around to pick up its passengers. Two miles away he found them stranded. The driver was frantically working on his engine trying to get it started.

Sam jumped out of his car. "Yo' all bettah get in here in a hurry," he said excitedly. "Come here, boy," he called to the driver, "and help me wif dese bags."

In a jiffy the four Castillios and their suitcases were transferred to the Bobbsey automobile. Sam got in behind the wheel, quickly turned the car around in the road, and headed back for the airport. Overhead he could see a plane preparing to come down.

He wondered if he could get there in time!

Back at the airport, the Bobbsey family was frantic. Mr. Bobbsey hurried to the main desk and asked if it would be possible to hold the plane a few minutes. He explained that something must have detained the Castillios. He mentioned how far they were going, and said it would be a shame for the plane to go off without them.

"It will take a few minutes to refuel," the man told him, "and after we are ready to leave, we will wait five minutes, but no longer," he added.

The plane landed. Ordinarily the Bobbsey twins would have been fascinated, watching the passengers come off and bags of mail being unloaded. It would have been exciting to see their own luggage go aboard, but now they were too worried to be interested. Every few seconds they would run to the door to see if their friends had come yet.

They did not know that old Sam was making the Bobbsey car go as fast as he dared, trying to get the Castillios there in time. A voice came over the loud-speaker:

"Flight Number 10 now ready. Passengers please go aboard."

A car raced up to the entrance. Mr. Castillio jumped out and rushed through the building.

"Please hold it," he called to the man in charge. "We are taking that plane."

All the Bobbseys were aboard but Mr. Bobbsey. He was just about to enter the cabin when he heard his friend's voice.

"They're here," he told the pilot who was just coming aboard. "Can you hold it a minute?"

The man smiled and said he would. One by one the Castillios hurried up the steps, out of breath, and boarded the plane. The great door was slammed shut and locked, and the engines began to roar. The plane taxied across the field and turned around.

Up in front, a little electric sign went on. It told the passengers to fasten their seat belts. A young woman in a uniform, the stewardess, came to show the small children how to strap themselves into the seats, but they already knew how. Freddie was disappointed, because he wanted to stand on the seat and see all he could of Lakeport as they took off. But now that he was strapped in, he could see practically nothing, although he had a window seat.

A moment later the plane started its run across the field at a fast clip. Then gracefully it left the ground. After the passengers had been in the air a few minutes the little electric sign went out. The friendly stewardess unfastened the children's belts for them. Now they looked down from the windows and watched Lakeport fast disappearing behind them.

As soon as the excitement of the take-off was over, the Bobbseys asked the Castillios what had happened to delay them. Mr. Castillio told them about the taxicab engine suddenly going dead, and how the driver had been unable to get it started. It was not until now that the Bobbseys learned that Sam had rescued their friends.

"I did not even have time to thank him," said Mr. Castillio. "Will you please be sure to do it for me?"

Nan said she planned to send a postal card to Dinah and Sam at the first airport at which they would stop, so she would send the message.

Lunch was served on board. The children enjoyed unwrapping the various packages of food which the stewardess served on cardboard trays. A picnic anywhere was fun, but to have one in the air seemed more fun than anywhere else. They had just finished eating when they heard a baby cry. The grownups as well as the children were startled. None of them had noticed a baby on board. Where was it?

Freddie, more curious than the others, hopped out of his seat and walked up and down the aisle. He did not see a baby anywhere. Still it kept on crying. It seemed to Freddie as if the crying came from the rear of the plane. As he stood there looking puzzled, the stewardess smiled at him.

"Have you got a baby hidden away in the baggage?" Freddie asked.

The young woman chuckled. "Why, no," she replied, "the baby is right here."

"But where?" Freddie asked.

By this time Flossie and Marina also had climbed out of their seats and joined Freddie. Everyone else in the plane was smiling and turning to look toward the rear.

"My gracious," said a woman sitting just in front of the stewardess, "my baby is very disturbing."

The small Bobbsey twins and Marina gazed at her. Then they looked all around the floor and in the rack above her seat. Certainly there was no baby to be seen.

Laughingly merrily, the woman leaned down and picked up a small suitcase near her feet. She laid it on her lap and raised the lid. The children's eyes were as big as saucers. They could not believe anyone would keep a baby in a suitcase!

There was no baby inside, but a beautifully dressed baby doll. The woman picked up the doll and showed the youngsters a little key that was hidden under its sweater. By winding it up, she could make the doll cry.

"I'm taking this to my little granddaughter," she explained. "I couldn't resist playing a joke on you."

The children thought the doll was wonderful. Even Freddie, who did not care for dolls, wanted to turn the key and make the doll cry. But the woman said she had disturbed the passengers enough and put the doll back into the suitcase.

In the early afternoon the plane came down at an airport near New York City. A big bus took them all into town. While Mr. Bobbsey went off to attend to some business, the twins' mother showed the Castillios and her children some of the interesting sights. Then they met Mr. Bobbsey again at the airport and had dinner there.

Freddie wanted to know if the plane they were to stay on all night had beds in it. Mrs. Bobbsey said it did not have real beds, but that the seats could be tilted back far enough so that one might sleep very comfortably in them.

When the Bobbseys and their friends were in the air again, the young travelers were interested in watching the lights below them. Sometimes there were a great many of them, sometimes only a few.

At one point they saw only a row of moving lights. Mr. Bobbsey said this was one of the big highways which ran through farm lands, and that the lights they saw were on cars and trucks.

"Those lights look as small as the ones on my toy train," said Freddie, yawning.

His mother tilted back her small son's chair. The stewardess tucked a little pillow under his head, and soon Freddie was asleep. Flossie smiled to think she had stayed awake longer than her twin, but within another minute she, too, was sound asleep. The next thing they knew someone was tapping them on the shoulder.

"Time to get up," their mother's voice said.

She began to adjust their seat belts. In a moment they were wide awake and knew they were going to land.

"Are we in Mexico?" Flossie asked.

"Not yet, dear," Mrs. Bobbsey replied. "We're in Texas."

Presently the landing wheels of the plane touched the ground and the pilot taxied the big aircraft toward the airport building.

This time Mrs. Bobbsey and Mrs. Castillio carried small suitcases from the plane and escorted their daughters to the ladies' waiting room. Here they washed and brushed their teeth, and patiently Flossie had her curls combed.

"You can even take a bath here, can't you?" the little girl remarked, seeing a shower stall in the place.

"Yes," laughed Mrs. Bobbsey. "There are all the comforts of home here for travelers."

When they went outside, they found the men and the boys on the field looking at an even bigger plane than the one which had brought them there. This was the plane which would carry them through the high mountains of Mexico and into the city where they were going to stay for a couple of weeks.

"Pilots have to be specially trained to fly among those mountains," said Mr. Bobbsey.

"You mean it's dangerous?" Bert asked him.

"It would be dangerous if you didn't know how," his father replied. "There are very few landing fields, and a pilot must know exactly how to wind his way in and out among the peaks."

Bert wanted to know why they did not fly up over them. Mr. Bobbsey said the mountains were so high it would take a special kind of plane to go above them; otherwise, the passengers would be uncomfortable in the high altitude.

"We'll be up eleven thousand feet as it is," he added.

"Whew!" said Bert.

Freddie and Flossie merely gaped. They could not figure out how high eleven thousand feet was.

"There's our chief pilot," Mr. Bobbsey pointed out, as a young, dark-skinned man went past them.

The twins looked at him in awe. He was the person who was going to take them safely in and out among the dangerous mountain peaks.

CHAPTER XVII

A NEAR ACCIDENT

"WE GOT in the clouds right away, didn't we, Daddy?" Flossie remarked twenty minutes after they had left the Texas airport.

The words were hardly out of her mouth, when the big plane came out of the white mass. The children looked down and saw that they were flying over very blue water, with white foam along the shore. They knew this probably was the froth from high waves, but from the air they looked like little ripples of water.

"When do we come to the mountains, Daddy?" Freddie asked his father.

"In a little while," Mr. Bobbsey replied. "We'll eat breakfast first."

The stewardess served them, and the children thought it was amazing that scrambled eggs and bacon could taste so good, though they had been cooked on land before the plane took off.

Freddie was the first to see the mountain peaks.

From that moment on everyone in the plane ceased talking. They sat looking out of the windows, awed by the beautiful scenery.

"It doesn't look real," Nan thought. "It's like stage scenery."

The hills and valleys below the plane took on a rusty green color. Trees and bushes could not be distinguished. It looked like one great mass over which Mother Nature had laid a great velvety cloth.

Now and then the travelers could see small houses and farms far below them. The children assumed these were called haciendas. Once they spied cattle. The animals looked no larger than those in Freddie's toy farm.

The mountains became higher and higher, and presently the plane was flying over some and alongside others. After a while the stewardess walked up to the children.

"In a minute you'll be able to see the Sleeping Lady," she announced.

The twins wondered what she meant, but soon the young woman pointed out a snow-capped mountain. A little later she pointed out another from the summit of which smoke was pouring.

"I'll tell you the legend about them," she said, and sat down on the arm of Nan's chair.

"Long, long ago a princess lived in the moon," the stewardess began. "It was her job to see that the light of the moon never went out. Now, one time the sun happened to be in the sky at the same time. On the sun lived a prince. When the sun prince and the moon princess saw each other, they fell in love.

" 'Oh, I must make a beautiful silver dress to wear for him,' thought the princess.

"She worked very hard to make it, sewing day and night. By the end of the third night the poor princess was so tired she fell asleep, and was not able to look after the light of the moon. It went out, and bad things began to happen on the earth.

"Now the king of the sky, who had charge of the sun and the moon, was very angry because the princess had gone to sleep. To punish her, he decreed that she would have to stay asleep for ten thousand years. He made her leave the moon, come down to the earth, and find a place in which to rest. She chose the top of a mountain which was named Ixtacihuatl (pronounced Eez-tah-see-waht'l).

"She has been lying there so long in her beautiful silver dress that snow has covered her," the stewardess finished the story.

"The poor princess!" exclaimed Flossie. "And what happened to the prince?"

"He decided to follow her. Popocatepetl, for that became his name (pronounced Poh-poh-kah-tay-pet'l), went to a near-by mountain. He built a great fire and sat there day after day, waiting for her to wake up."

Freddie asked when the princess would wake up, and was told it would not be for at least another five thousand years. The little boy also wanted to know if they could go to see the prince.

"Oh, no one ever sees him." The stewardess smiled. "But don't worry, there'll be many other interesting things for you to see in Mexico."

The wonderful trip seemed all too short to the Bobbseys. Actually, it was slightly longer than it would have been if the plane had followed the most direct route. Instead, its course was charted so as to include a good view of the two famous mountains. Now the pilot was circling the airport, and when he got the clearance signal to land, brought his big plane down. The next thing the Bobbsey twins knew, the cabin door opened, and they were climbing down the steps. They were in Mexico!

The small twins looked all around, and wondered where the beautiful city was which they had thought they were going to visit. All they could see were the airport buildings and acres and acres of flat fields. They learned that the city was several miles away.

It was at this airport that the Bobbseys would say good-bye to the Castillios. They were changing to another plane which would carry them directly to their hacienda.

"We will expect to see you in about two weeks," Mrs. Castillio smiled, shaking hands. "I hope you have a very pleasant vacation here."

The twins were sorry to see Mateo and Marina leave. They had played with them almost every day for the past few weeks, and it would seem strange not to be with them.

At first, the Bobbsey children did not think this airport very different from the other airports at which they had landed. But a moment later they changed their minds. A voice over the loud-speaker spoke in Spanish. Then on every side they began to hear the foreign language. Bert wished now that he had studied Spanish as his sister had done. Every few seconds he would ask her what the people were talking about.

Nan grinned. "I wish they wouldn't speak so fast. I can't understand half of what they're saying."

As soon as the Bobbseys' luggage was off the plane, they hailed a taxi. The driver looked at them and at the bags. "You need two taxi," he said in English.

He beckoned to another man, and the family and the bags were divided. But the cars followed each other along the road that led into Mexico City.

On the way the twins saw a strange combination of the old way of doing things and modern methods. An up-to-date automobile would hurry past a man leading a burro, with large bundles of wood strapped on its sides.

As they came into the city, the children found the streets narrow. The low buildings were close together, and looked as if they were made of pink plaster. Nan liked best those that were decorated with blue paint.

Many people were on the streets. Some were dressed just like the people in Lakeport; others, whom the twins knew were Indians, looked like those who live on reservations in the United States. The women had on long, embroidered skirts, and wore shawls over their blouses. Many of the men had long black hair woven in braids down their backs.

One of the things the Bobbseys did notice especially was that everyone was dressed for warm weather. The air was very clear and the sunshine bright.

"The people even have sunshine in their eyes," Flossie told her mother, with whom she was riding. As the taxi stopped for a traffic signal, many of the passers-by smiled at her. "And they're friendly, too," she added.

The taxi driver turned around. "You are right, *Niña*," he said to her. "Mexicans are happy people. They have sunshine in their eyes and in their hearts."

He started his car again, and soon they came to a beautiful part of the city. The streets were wider, the buildings large and attractive. They went past a cathedral that was the largest church the children had ever seen, and they were told it was one of the oldest in America.

They drove along a tree-shaded avenue with a

parkway in the center, and in a little while drew up in front of a hotel. Two bellhops ran down the steps, took their bags, and led them into the lobby. What an attractive place it was!

Large potted palms stood here and there, and bouquets of bright-colored flowers were everywhere. To the twins' surprise, English was being spoken as much as Spanish. Bert began to feel more at home.

"I guess most everybody here speaks English," he told himself, "so it's all right I didn't learn Spanish."

But when they got upstairs to their rooms he thought differently. A chambermaid, who had just finished making the beds, could not speak a word of English. She smiled sweetly and said something to the children. Nan smiled back, and spoke to her in Spanish. The young woman's black eyes sparkled, and there was laughter in her voice as they conversed slowly. Nan told Bert the chambermaid had said how pretty all the children were.

"Humph!" said the boy. "How do I know she said that? Maybe you're just making it up."

Nan, seeing a chance to tease her twin, merely remarked that if Bert did not want her to translate for him, then she would not bother. Bert did not know what to do. He didn't want to miss anything, yet he did not want his sister to pretend she knew everything that was being said, even though she might not.

He walked out of the room and went into the bedroom which he would share with Freddie. Mr. and Mrs. Bobbsey were to have the girls on one side of them and the boys on the other. On Nan's bureau was a large bouquet of flowers. Nan remarked about them to the chambermaid.

"Everyone in Mexico loves flowers," the young woman told her, "and they bloom all the time. Do you have lots of flowers where you live?"

Nan said that where she lived it was not possible to have flowers outdoors except in warm weather because of the snow and cold. The rest of the year they had flowering plants indoors.

The chambermaid remarked she had never seen snow except from a distance on top of the mountain outside of the city. She had never felt of it, nor played in it.

"But I've seen moving pictures of it," the young woman said. "Maybe I'll come to your country someday and ride in the snow."

After the children had hung up their clothes, they begged to go outdoors and see more of the city. Mr. Bobbsey said there was just time enough for all of them to go for a walk before dinner.

When they reached the street, Bert became interested in some construction work on an apartment house. He ran ahead of the others to gaze up at the workmen. Small iron balconies with low railings were being built in front of the second-floor windows.

On one a flower box with flowers already growing in it was being set in place. Bert stood directly beneath it, but he was not so much interested in that as he was in watching two men who were putting another railing in place along the side of the building.

Suddenly the heavy flower box began to teeter! The man holding it tried to grab the box but was not able to pull it back into place.

"Cuidado!" someone yelled at Bert, seeing the boy standing under the flower box.

But Bert did not understand the warning given in Spanish. He stood still as the workman lost hold of the heavy box!

CHAPTER XVIII

THE FLOATING GARDENS

NAN BOBBSEY had started walking toward her brother. Hearing the workmen's warning, she looked up to see what the trouble was. At this very moment the flower box toppled from the balcony!

"Look out, Bert!" the girl screamed. "Look out!"

Her twin jumped aside only a second before the box crashed to the sidewalk.

"Oh!" he gasped, startled.

The man above him began to speak rapidly in Spanish. Nan caught a few words, and knew he was apologizing to Bert. Then he uttered a prayer of thanks that no one had been hurt.

The other Bobbseys had heard the crash, but they did not know that Nan had saved her brother from being injured. When Bert told them about it, they praised her because she had recognized the Spanish word of warning and called out to her twin.

Bert ruefully remarked, as he looked at the broken

flowers lying on the sidewalk, that he would never forget Nan's quick thinking.

"Thanks a lot, Nan," he added.

"If you haven't lost your taste for flowers, Bert," Mrs. Bobbsey said, laughing, "someday we'll all go to see the beautiful gardenia pool. Can you imagine anything more lovely than swimming in a pond with gardenias floating on the surface?" she asked, as they walked back to the hotel.

"May we go to the floating gardens too?" Nan asked.

"Yes, tomorrow," Mr. Bobbsey promised. "Now we'll go to dinner."

The twins were very much interested in the hotel menu. One side of it was printed in Spanish, the other in English. By the end of the meal Flossie had learned that *leche* meant milk, and decided that while she was in Mexico she would always ask for leche.

The following morning was as beautiful as the day before had been. The twins were told that, except during the rainy season, which is from June to October, every day in Mexico City is clear and warm.

"I wish it would be that way in Lakeport," sighed Nan. "Sometimes it's warm when we go to school and cold when we come home. And lots of times it rains in the morning and then we have to carry our raincoats home at noontime."

Mrs. Bobbsey said that if they lived in Mexico

City it certainly would be easier for her and Dinah to
see that the children wore the proper clothes.

After breakfast they all set out by car for the
floating gardens. On the way Manuel, their young
driver and guide, who spoke very good English, told
them a little of the history of Mexico.

"People have lived in Mexico a long, long time,"
he said, "but only Indians were here until four hundred years ago. Then the Spanish came."

As Manuel drove on, he pointed out a vast area
which he said had once been a lake.

"Where did the water go?" Freddie asked him.

"We drained it out," the driver replied. "There's
a story that when the Spanish came here, the ruler of
the Indians, who was named Montezuma, had a
great deal of gold. When he found that the Spanish
were going to steal it, he ordered it thrown into the
lake. A few years ago some of my countrymen
thought it would be a fine idea to find the gold. We
could use it to educate our people and build many
nice buildings for them. So we drained all the water
out of the lake, and people have been digging for
gold ever since."

"Did they find the gold?" Freddie asked, his eyes
big as saucers.

The young man shook his head. "Oh, we have
found some here and there. But we have not found
as much as Montezuma had."

The twins exclaimed that it would be wonderful to find a great treasure. Freddie and Flossie would have liked to get out of the car at once and start digging, but their parents laughed and said that probably after four hundred years the gold had sunk far down in the mud. It would be only by accident that anyone would find the treasure.

"It must have been beautiful here when there was a lake," commented Mrs. Bobbsey. "I presume the Indians sailed on it in canoes."

Manuel said he had heard that those ancient canoes were very, very strong, and could carry heavy loads. All the big stones in the pyramids had been carried from the mountains across the lake to the place where the pyramids had been built.

"Nowadays we cannot figure out how the people did it," Manuel said.

When they reached the floating gardens, the young man explained that once upon a time this place, too, had been a lake. Certain Indians, in order to be safe from their enemies, lived on rafts on the water. They brought soil, and in it planted vegetables and flowers. The roots of various plants grew down through the rafts and into the water. After a while the gardens became little islands.

"We will take a boat and go in and out among the islands," said Manuel.

There were many boats and many men, all calling

out, each boatman hoping the Bobbseys would choose his boat. Some had roofs, and all were decorated with flowers. A few had arched frames twined with flowers, and even had names made of flowers. Flossie chose one of these called *Lolita*.

The Bobbsey family and Manuel climbed in and seated themselves on chairs. A barefoot man standing at the end of the boat pushed off from shore with a long pole. Laying down the pole, he started the motor, and steered carefully. There were so many boats coming and going that he had to be careful not to bump into them.

Everyone seemed to be in holiday mood. People were singing to the accompaniment of guitars and violins. Here and there were small boats, from which natives were selling flowers, food, and drinks. When the Bobbseys came to one where Indian women were cooking food, Freddie suddenly was sure he was hungry. As they passed a boat filled with ice and bottles of pop, he said he was thirsty. Mrs. Bobbsey, however, suggested that Freddie wait until they had completed their trip.

As they rounded the corner of one of the islands, on which beautiful white flowers were growing, they came upon a smiling Indian woman in a long dugout. Her entire canoe was covered with enormous violets. Mrs. Bobbsey could not resist them, and purchased a big bouquet of the beautiful blue flowers.

The *Lolita* now headed out into the middle of the stream, where a boatload of musicians seemed to be waiting for the Bobbseys. The twins were fascinated by the musicians' costumes. They wore the biggest hats the children had ever seen. The leader of the group had on one which was as wide as his shoulders, and went up to a point two feet above his head. It was made of black felt, and was trimmed with strings of red tassels. His coat, made of black satin, was tight fitting. Narrow strips of gold braid trimmed the front. The man had a long, flowing, black mustache.

His companions also wore large hats, but these were made of light-colored straw. The men played guitars, while the leader played a violin. All of them sang. Most of the songs were gay dance tunes. Flossie could not resist doing a few steps in the rear of the boat. This pleased Manuel, and he began to sing with the men.

Manuel had a fine tenor voice, and when the other musicians heard him, they immediately stopped singing, and gave him a chance to sing a solo. When he reached the chorus, he motioned the Bobbseys to join in, but only Nan did. In school she had learned the tune with English words, but Anita had taught her the song in Spanish. Manuel was extremely pleased and the men in the other boat, hearing her, clapped when she had finished. Nan blushed, but was happy.

Mr. Bobbsey gave the musicians some money, and the travelers went on to see more of the gardens. Freddie decided a little later that they must be on their way back when he saw the Indian woman with the violets again.

"Now I can have something to drink," he announced. Turning to Manuel, he said, "Please, will you ask the boatman to find me a pop boat?"

In a couple of minutes they drew alongside of one, and Freddie was allowed a bottle of pop. Everyone had some, and all were so busy with the ice-cold drink that they did not notice what Freddie was doing. Having seen the Mexican boatmen in bare feet, he decided this must be the thing to do. Quickly he removed his shoes and socks. Then he decided he would like to put his feet in the water.

Freddie sat down on the edge of the boat, and tried to reach the water with his feet. But, alas, he lost his balance!

Plop! Freddie Bobbsey had fallen into the waters of the floating gardens!

"Oh!" cried Nan, who had looked up just in time to see her small brother go overboard.

Freddie could swim enough not to be frightened in water. He quickly came to the surface and his father pulled him aboard. His mother wondered what to do about him, for his clothes were soaking wet.

"Do not worry about him," Manuel smiled kindly. "He will not catch cold in this warm air. We will hurry back to the dock and dry his clothes quickly."

When they reached the dock, Manuel took Freddie off to a near-by restaurant. While the others were waiting, they shopped among the stands near the dock. The children were fascinated by the Indian blankets, baskets, jewelry, and pocketbooks. Of them all, the girls were most interested in the pocketbooks. These were made of alligator skin. Some of them had part of the alligator's foot as a decoration.

Twenty minutes later Manuel and Freddie reappeared, and no one would have known anything had happened to Freddie. His clothes not only were dry, but they had been neatly pressed.

"This is a most amazing country," Mrs. Bobbsey said. "I have heard of your duendes. I believe you must have some of them right here!"

Manuel smiled. "Maybe one of them is a laundress for the restaurant!"

Bert had wandered off to a corner where a man was selling various kinds of tiny animals. Among them were horned toads—those strange little toads with spikes on their bodies and horns on their heads. There were also baby alligators and chameleons. The man put one of the chameleons on Bert's shoulder.

Freddie, fascinated, watched the tiny lizard as it slowly turned the color of his brother's coat. He wanted to buy one to take home to Sam, but his mother was afraid Dinah would not like Sam to have the lizard.

"We'll find something else to take home to him and Dinah," Mrs. Bobbsey said.

Mr. Bobbsey had been looking at the various articles himself, as he wanted to surprise his wife and daughters with gifts. When they were seated in the automobile once more, he handed each of them a little package.

CHAPTER XIX

FLYING FEATHERS!

EAGERLY Mrs. Bobbsey and the two girls opened their packages. The boys looked on enviously because they had received no gifts. But they said nothing, knowing that sooner or later their father would give them something.

"Oh, what a beautiful bracelet!" the twins' mother exclaimed.

She held up a silver bracelet fashioned in the form of a curled-up snake. It had pieces of green jade for eyes, and Mrs. Bobbsey declared they almost looked real. She slipped the bracelet on her wrist and, as she thanked her husband, said it was one of the loveliest Mexican bracelets she had ever seen.

By this time Nan and Flossie had their packages open. They, too, had silver bracelets made by the Indians. Each one had an animal ornament in the center. Nan's was an iguana and she wondered if she would see one of these lizards while she was in Mexico.

Flossie's bracelet had a crocodile on it. She asked her father where the real crocodiles were, and he laughingly replied that they were a safe distance away. He also told her that silver is found in great quantities in the mountains of Mexico. Although the Bobbseys could not go to any of the mines on this trip, he planned to take them to a silver factory. The twins wanted to go to the factory at once, so when they got back to Mexico City, Manuel took them to one.

As the children entered the building they saw room after room of beautiful silver objects. They had seen pieces like some of them in Lakeport, but in looking around, they came upon others which were quite new to them. One was a pointed hat two feet wide and a foot and a half high.

"Wow!" cried Freddie. "Who's going to wear that hat? A singing man at the floating gardens?"

A young woman who came to wait on them answered him in English:

"No one is going to wear it. It is to be used as a prize," she explained. "In your country, I believe you use cups, but here the athletes sometimes receive a silver hat."

Freddie found some tiny silver hats which were just the same shape as the big one, and Mr. Bobbsey bought him one. Then they went on to the back of the building, where the articles were made. The chil-

dren were warned not to go too close to the stoves
on which the huge pots of liquid silver were boiling.

"Come and see what these men are making,"
Manuel called, and led them to a corner of the factory.

At first the twins could not figure out what the
small figures were. They looked like little men, but
they were not dressed in regular clothes. Finally the
workman who was polishing one of the silver figures
finished his job and stood the figure up on the palm
of his hand.

"Oh, I know what it is!" Flossie cried out. "It's a
duende!"

The silversmith smiled at her. He could not speak
English, but he was pleased that she knew it was a
duende. He spoke to Manuel in Spanish. Nan smiled
because she could understand him and was pleased
at what he was saying.

"Ask the boss if he will sell this cheap to the little
girl," the workman had said.

Manuel looked at Nan and said to her in Spanish,
"Suppose you and I go find the boss."

The other Bobbseys wondered what was happening as the two hurried away. Flossie now was holding
the silver duende and saying that it was a better-
looking elf than any of the little men who lived on
the showboat. This reminded her again that the
Bobbseys were supposed to find some midgets for

Captain Friday Night's traveling amusement park.

In a minute Manuel and Nan came back with the manager of the silver factory. He was a pleasant man, and he was smiling broadly. Addressing Mr. Bobbsey, he said:

"I understand you are an unusually fortunate man; you have two sets of twins in your family. That in itself makes me want to ask you to accept a little souvenir from my factory. Now, I believe one of your children recognized my Mexican duende. That gives me great happiness, and I should like very much to present this silver elf to your little girl."

Flossie's eyes grew very round. For a second she was afraid her father might not let her accept the gift, because she had been told never to accept gifts from strangers. She hugged the little silver figure tightly as she waited for Mr. Bobbsey to speak.

"Your kindness is very great," he replied, smiling. "It is true that I am a very lucky father. Have you children, too?" he asked.

The manager's answer was rather amazing. "I have twelve children," he said, "with two sets of twins, so you see why I have a special reason for asking you to accept a gift from me."

Flossie was allowed to keep the silver duende. She thanked the manager and told him how she hoped to see some real duendes in a Mexican forest. The factory manager chuckled and said that he hoped she would not be disappointed, but in any case she would have the silver duende to remind her of the little forest people.

Mr. and Mrs. Bobbsey bought several articles in the store. Most of these were to take back to their friends in Lakeport. But they also picked out an attractive fruit bowl to give the Castillios.

That night, when the children were ready to go upstairs to bed, Nan asked her father where he was going to take them the next morning.

"Manuel suggests we go to one of the towns a few miles from here," he replied. "It will be market day there tomorrow, and he thinks it will be fun to see."

The twins and their parents started off early the next day. Manuel said that they would see Indians on the road who were taking their wares to sell at the market place. When he told the twins how many miles some of the Indians walked to get to market, they were amazed.

"They start the night before," Manuel explained. "They have burros to carry their loads, but the Indians themselves rarely ride."

After an hour's drive the Bobbseys began to see Indians going to the market place. Most of them were men, but now and then they would see women and children. Their burros were carrying such big loads that Nan wondered why the poor little animals did not fall right down in the road. She learned that they are amazingly strong and sturdy, and are better at climbing hills and following narrow paths than horses are.

The burros' loads included so many kinds of things that the twins began to play a game to see who could count the most. By the time they came near the town where the market place was, Bert had counted twenty-five different articles! But what amazed the children the most were the live chickens. These were sometimes carried in crates strapped to each side of the burros. Once, however, they saw ten live roosters, their feet bound together, hanging upside down from the sides of one of the little animals.

"They must be well-trained chickies," Flossie remarked. "They don't bite each other and they don't bite the burro."

Manuel laughed. "I guess if you had ridden upside down for twenty miles you wouldn't feel much like biting anything."

"Oh, the poor chickies!" the little girl exclaimed. She pleaded with her father to stop so she could speak to the Indian woman who was walking beside the burro. Flossie wanted to ask her to let the roosters loose for a little while, but Mr. Bobbsey thought his small daughter merely wanted to get out and have a better look at the unusual sight.

Flossie hopped out and spoke to the Indian. The

woman did not understand English, but she thought the people in the car wanted to buy her roosters. Manuel got out and spoke to her in Spanish, and the Indian did not speak Spanish either. But now she was sure they wanted her roosters.

Quickly the woman untied five of the roosters. Holding them by the feet, she came over to the automobile. Before anyone realized what was happening, she put the roosters into the back of the car and closed the doors.

"Oh!" cried Mrs. Bobbsey.

The twins' mother leaned over to open the door, but before she could do so, the roosters, far from being exhausted, started to fly around the car!

CHAPTER XX

THE STRANGE MARKET

AS the Bobbseys in the back of the automobile tried to dodge the excited roosters, Mr. Bobbsey hopped out of the front seat. He quickly opened the doors on his side of the car, and shoved out two of the roosters. Manuel opened the doors on the other side and got hold of two more. In the meantime, Mrs. Bobbsey and the twins climbed out, and Bert raced across a field after the fifth.

By this time the Indian woman understood that they did not want to buy her roosters. When all the birds had been captured and handed back to her, she tied them up and fastened them once more to the side of the burro. For a moment she stared sulkily at the Bobbseys, then walked on down the road.

"Well, of all things!" said Mrs. Bobbsey, looking after the Indian woman. "Do you suppose she is angry because we didn't buy her live roosters?"

Manuel believed she was. He said it was very difficult to trade with some of the Indians because they did not speak Spanish. Nevertheless, they knew all about Mexican money and were good traders.

"Oh, look!" cried Freddie, and pointed to a barefoot boy about as tall as Bert.

The lad was walking along the dusty road, trying to guide a flock of turkeys with a whip. Each time one of them would get out of line, he would flick it on the neck with his whip.

"Are they going to market too?" Freddie asked Manuel.

"Yes," said their guide. "Indians, and in fact most Mexicans, like to buy their poultry alive. Then they know it is fresh. In the country they have no ice and not many people have electric refrigerators, so they cannot keep food fresh very long."

The car had to be driven slowly for a few minutes, because one of the turkeys kept getting out of line and running in front of the automobile. The turkey boy finally gave it a harder flick with his whip. Squawking, the turkey got out of the way of the car and Manuel was able to drive a little faster.

A few minutes later they reached the town and parked a short distance from the market place. The streets were full of people, some of them carrying things to sell and others carrying away various articles they had bought. Manuel said it was hard to tell whether they were coming or going.

Presently the children spied a man who was balancing a stack of straw hats on his head. There were at least twenty of them, and the twins wondered how in the world he could keep them from toppling over.

"Is he a before or after man?" Flossie asked.

"What do you mean, dear?" her mother asked, smiling.

Flossie wanted to know whether the man was carrying the hats to the market to sell or whether he had bought them and was taking them home. Manuel was sure the fellow had woven the hats himself and hoped to sell them.

"I think we ought to buy one for Sam," announced Freddie. "He always wears a hat, Daddy, when he works in your lumberyard."

Mr. Bobbsey said that was true, but he doubted that Sam would want one of the high-pointed hats. Manuel said he knew a place in Mexico City where they made straw hats like the ones worn in the United States. He promised to take Freddie there, so he might purchase one for Sam.

It seemed to the Bobbseys as if the Indians carried everything on their heads. One old man came along with an enormous basket perched on top of his head. In it were piled fruits of various kinds. Many of these the children had never seen. They included guavas, cactus pears, and mangoes.

Manuel suggested that they follow the old man,

but this was hard work. As the Bobbseys entered the market place they found it difficult to make their way through it. The place was shaded by a white canvas roof. Booths and counters were set up here and there, but there seemed to be no definite streets in the place. The Indians who had no booths were sitting on the ground. Around them were their bright-eyed children and the things they had brought to sell. Many of the women were cooking. Manuel pointed toward one of them.

"She is making *tortillas*," he said. "They are white corn-meal pancakes."

"I'd like those," said Freddie.

Manuel laughingly answered, "I'm sure you wouldn't like what they roll up in them."

He explained that as many different things could go inside of a rolled-up tortilla as people in the United States put inside sandwiches.

"But some of the combinations burn your tongue, Freddie," the guide said.

The twins noticed that the young Indian woman had made little heaps of food on a large wooden platter. Some of these were salads made of cut-up cactus leaves and fruit. In the others were chopped peppers, onions, or pork. Holding a hot tortilla on the palm of one hand, she dotted it with bits of the various foods on the platter. Then with her other hand she quickly rolled up the tortilla. Now it was ready to eat. Smiling, she held it toward Freddie.

"You buy?" she said.

"Better not," advised Manuel. "Later I shall take you to a restaurant where you can have a tortilla."

Freddie was a little disappointed, but he had grown fond of Manuel and realized that he knew best. The Bobbseys wound their way in and out among the displays in the market place. There were many beautiful flowers for sale and Mrs. Bobbsey bought some gardenias. The woman who sold the flowers insisted that Nan put one in her hair.

"There's the fruit man," Bert spoke up.

The twins went over to watch the old man set up his display. It seemed impossible that anyone could have carried so much on his head. He had set down his huge basket, and now was on his knees arranging small baskets of the fruit in front of him. When he finished he had eight of them! And each basket actually was piled high with fruit!

Bert grinned. "He's a magician! Instead of pulling rabbits out of a hat, he must have pulled fruit out of his head!"

Manuel pointed to a string of short, fancy sticks hanging from a red cord stretched across the front of one of the stalls. He asked if the twins knew what these were for. They had never seen any before, and neither had Mr. or Mrs. Bobbsey.

Each stick was attractively carved. At one end was a round ball with crisscrossed threads of silver for decoration.

"They are for stirring chocolate," Manuel said. "You know we drink a great deal of chocolate in Mexico."

"We do, too," said Flossie, "but we always stir it with a spoon."

"I think these are prettier than spoons," Nan remarked. "Mother, I'd like to buy some to take home to my friends." Mrs. Bobbsey thought that was a good idea and she, too, bought a few.

In the meantime, Bert and Freddie had walked away from the others. They had seen a boy coming into the market place with a cage and were curious to see what kind of animal was inside. From where they were, they could see that the animal was pacing restlessly in its prison.

Suddenly there were excited exclamations from the Indians in the market place. Bert and Freddie could not understand what they were saying, but thought it must be about the animal, because some of the Indians were pointing to it.

The Indian boy who was carrying the cage paid no attention. As the boy came closer, Bert saw that the animal was a bobcat. He knew that bobcats are vicious, and that the animal would scratch and bite if it should get loose.

As the Indian boy came near them, a man spoke angrily to him. Bert was sure he was ordering the boy to take the dangerous animal away. When the boy did not make a move to leave, the man grabbed the cage.

As he started off with it, the Indian boy grabbed the cage back. In the tussle which followed between him and the man, the cage fell to the ground. The door came open and the bobcat jumped out.

People screamed and tried to run to safety. Snarling, the bobcat leaped. Bert and Freddie were directly in its path!

CHAPTER XXI

THE MIRACLE ARTIST

"CUIDADO!"

"Caramba!"

These and similar cries of warning came from the crowd in the market place, as the vicious bobcat sprang toward Bert and Freddie Bobbsey. Like a flash Bert leaped aside, yanking Freddie with him.

The boys were safe for the moment, but the angry bobcat, as soon as it landed on the ground, turned around to spring again. The Indians and others in the market place were terrified. Poor Freddie was knocked down. He might have been trampled on, but at this moment a single voice roared above the noise of the crowd. Instantly everyone stood still in his place. A second later a shot rang out.

Then the babble of voices started again. The Bobbsey boys did not know what it was all about, but they did not wait to find out. Bert grabbed Freddie's hand and pushed through the crowd toward the place where he had left his parents. Every-

170

thing had happened so quickly Mr. and Mrs. Bobbsey had not known where to look for their sons in
the excited crowd of people.

"Are you all right?" their mother asked anxiously.

"Sure," said Freddie stoutly, "but he was an awful big, bad cat."

It was not until Manuel questioned various people
that they learned the whole story. The old man who
had carried the huge basket of fruit on his head was
the person who had saved Bert and Freddie from
injury. He had been the one who had ordered everyone to stand still, then had shot the angry bobcat.

The only person who was displeased about this
was the boy who had brought the animal to market.
He had hoped to sell it and get enough money to buy
some nice things for himself. None of the Mexicans
seemed to feel sorry for him. But the Bobbsey twins,
seeing how poorly he was dressed and how unhappy
he looked, offered to help him. The barefoot Indian
youth could speak neither English nor Spanish, and
they had a hard time making him understand what
they wished to do.

Freddie thought the boy should have some shoes,
so he pointed to his own shoes, then to the other's
bare feet. Finally the Indian understood, but shook
his head violently. Manuel said the boy probably
never had had a pair of shoes on his feet and much
preferred to walk around barefoot.

One by one the children pointed to the various articles of clothing for sale, but it seemed that the boy was not interested in any of them. At last Mrs. Bobbsey made motions as if she were eating, then pointed at the Indian's mouth. Now the lad grinned, so Mr. Bobbsey handed him some money. The last they saw of him he was eating tortillas and munching a mango.

The twins, seeing and smelling so much food, began to feel hungry. Manuel drove them to an attractive wayside restaurant. Part of it was outdoors in a garden where all sorts of parrots perched in the trees and chattered at the guests. The other part of the restaurant was in a cave. Freddie thought it would be more fun to eat in there and pretend he was one of the people who lived in Mexico long, long ago and had his home in a cave.

In the end the family was divided. Manuel took the two boys into the cave. Mr. and Mrs. Bobbsey and the girls remained in the lovely garden. When they were about halfway through their meal a young man with long hair walked into the garden and came up to the twins' father. He was carrying a paintbox and brushes. In Spanish he said to Mr. Bobbsey:

"Are you not the Señor whose sons were saved from the bobcat?"

Mr. Bobbsey smiled and said he did not understand Spanish. He asked the young man to speak in English, but the artist shook his head to show he could not.

"Oh, I know what he said, Daddy," Nan spoke up. To the young man she said, *"Si."*

"Where are the boys of your family?" he asked her.

Nan pointed toward the cave. The man now explained to Nan what he wanted, but her knowledge of Spanish was not yet good enough for her to make out what he was saying.

"You'd better talk to Manuel," she said in Spanish. "Please follow me."

She hurried into the cave and asked the guide to find out what the young man wanted. After listening to him a few minutes, Manuel explained that he was a "miracle artist."

"Whenever a person is saved from injury, it is good luck for him to have his picture painted," he said. "It is good luck for the artist, too. This man wants to know if the boys would like their picture painted."

Bert and Freddie thought it might be fun. They could take it home to show their friends in Lakeport. Bert hurried to the garden to ask his parents. Mr. Bobbsey asked what the charge would be and gave his consent.

The young man posed the boys in front of the cave. Then he walked off a short distance, sat down

on the ground, and opened his paintbox. Holding a
canvas in front of him, he began to sketch the picture. Freddie managed to keep still for a few minutes. Just as he was becoming fidgety and was sure
he would have to stand up, the young man announced
he had finished.

Freddie dashed over to look at the picture. His
eyes nearly popped from his head. He expected to see
a portrait of himself and Bert in front of the cave.
Instead, the artist had made an exact duplicate of the
scene in the market place. In the background were
Indians in their bright-colored costumes. In the center of the picture were Bert and Freddie with the
bobcat leaping toward them.

"That's swell!" exclaimed Bert.

The other Bobbseys and Manuel complimented
the artist on his work. He had painted the background of the picture before leaving the market
place. All he had to do was to fill in the figures of
the boys, and each was a very good likeness. The
young artist said he had had a hard time finding out
where they had gone, but he was glad he had found
them.

Mr. Bobbsey was so pleased with the picture that
he gave the artist more money than he had asked.
The young man said he would put it into a fund he
was saving for a trip to the United States.

Nan told him in Spanish that she hoped he would enjoy his visit to her country as much as she was enjoying her trip to his. After he had gone, the Bobbseys finished their luncheon and then drove back to the hotel. Bert and Freddie proudly set the picture of themselves and the bobcat on their bureau. As Freddie got into bed later that evening, he still could see the picture and studied it more carefully. All was quiet for a while, then it seemed as if the bobcat suddenly came to life.

"Oh!" screamed Freddie.

"What's the matter with you?" he heard Bert's voice asking.

"The bo—bo—the—bob—bobcat is coming after me!" Freddie cried out.

He heard a laugh, and the next instant he was looking up at his brother, and the sun was shining brightly into the bedroom.

"Golly," said Bert, "you must have had an awful dream."

Freddie turned his eyes toward the bureau. There stood the picture of himself, Bert, and the bobcat. Sheepishly the small boy grinned.

"I—I thought that old bobcat was coming after us again," he said.

He hopped out of bed, because he remembered that this was the morning the twins were going to school in Mexico. Manuel had asked them the night before if they would like to go, and the twins had all agreed that it would be fun.

"Do the boys and girls go to school all day?" Nan asked Manuel a little later, as they drove toward the school.

"No, they come at eight and leave at one," he told her.

When they arrived, Manuel parked the car and they walked up to the iron gate set in the high cement wall that hid the school building. Manuel rang a bell. Presently a pleasant-faced woman came and opened the gate.

The twins found themselves in a stone-paved courtyard. Opening off it were the classrooms of the one-story building. The rooms had only three walls. The sides facing the courtyard were entirely open.

"It's like having school outdoors," Flossie whispered to Nan. "I wish ours was like that."

They could see girls of various ages in the rooms, and were rather amazed that they did not turn around and look at the visitors. Each day the twins were becoming more conscious of the politeness and good behavior of Mexican children.

The young woman who had opened the gate led the Bobbseys and Manuel to the office of the head-mistress. She was delighted to meet the boys and girls from the United States, and was pleased to learn that one of them already was able to speak some Spanish. She herself spoke excellent English.

Smiling at the Bobbseys she said, "Suppose we go out into the courtyard and sit down. It is time for our dancing class. The girls will show you some of our native dances."

A few minutes later the older students came out dressed in colorful costumes. In a small room on the side a teacher played the piano for them. The Bobbsey twins thought the dances were wonderful. They were different from anything they had ever seen. The visitors were amazed that the children could dance so fast, yet never make a mistake.

The dance the boys liked best was the one where the music would suddenly stop and the dancers would stand still, looking at one another. Then one of the girls would call out and another would answer. All of them would laugh and the music would go on.

"What are they saying?" Bert asked his sister.

"They are making up jokes," she replied, laughing.

Bert kept insisting that she tell him what it was all about, but after he heard, he wished Nan had not told him. The dancers were making flattering remarks about Bert, and asking one another if they thought he would dance with any of them. Bert's face turned red, and he was glad when the music stopped and the girls left the courtyard.

The headmistress took the visitors from room to room. They found that the schoolwork was about the same as in Lakeport but in addition, the Mexican girls were taught to embroider. They were glad to show their work. Nan was amazed to see bedspreads and tablecloths, all beautifully embroidered by girls no older than herself.

"They're lovely!" she exclaimed in Spanish. "Will you sell these?" she asked two of the girls.

"Oh, no," one of them replied. "We shall save them until we marry."

As usual, Freddie became a little bored with so many girls. There were no boys at this school. Flossie was not very much interested in the embroidery. When her twin suggested they look around by themselves, she was glad to follow him.

The headmistress now asked the teacher of the class to have the girls sing. The pupils stood up and sang several Mexican songs, then one of the girls raised her hand and asked if the children from Lakeport would sing some songs for them in English. Bert was embarrassed, but Nan said they would be glad to do this. She and her brother sang *Swanee River, The Snow Man,* and *The Star-Spangled Banner.*

When the headmistress finally led the older Bobbsey twins from the classroom, Bert and Nan suddenly noticed that Freddie and Flossie were not with them. They asked Manuel where they were but he did not know.

"Oh, dear," said Nan, "I hope they're not in any mischief."

Manuel and Bert went one way, while Nan and the woman went another, looking for the small twins. They looked in classrooms and went to the office. Freddie and Flossie could not be found. The headmistress became concerned. Hurrying from room to room, she asked all the children if they had seen the young visitors. In the last classroom one of the pupils told her that she had seen the small twins near the entrance gate.

"They must have gone out into the street!" she exclaimed, worried, and hurried to the gate.

Nan and Bert followed her. The three of them looked up and down the street. Freddie and Flossie were not in sight.

"Oh," wailed Nan, "if my little brother and sister are lost in this city, we'll never be able to find them!"

CHAPTER XXII

THE DUENDES

THE headmistress of the school was now very much worried. Manuel was frantic. He had had charge of Freddie and Flossie, and now they were gone!

Manuel and the woman spoke rapidly in Spanish. Nan could not follow everything they said, but she understood a word here and there, and knew that they were going to notify the police.

Bert was trying very hard to think what there was near by which might have attracted his small brother and sister. Scanning the buildings across the street, the boy saw one which he felt sure they should investigate. It was a candy shop.

"Manuel," he said, "will you go across the street with me? I think Freddie and Flossie may be in the candy shop."

Manuel thought that Bert probably was right. The two of them hurried across the street, and looked in through the open door of the shop. Bert had guessed correctly. There stood Freddie with a peppermint stick in one hand and a number of caramels in the other. Flossie had an apple-shaped marzipan in one hand, and in the other was a tiny candy doll.

Behind the counter was a stout lady who wore a big white apron. Her black hair was pulled up tightly on her head and pinned in a knot. She could not speak English, and was finding it difficult to trade with her small customers. Freddie and Flossie had a few United States coins and the woman seemed willing to accept them, but she did not know how much the pieces of silver were worth. Manuel arrived just in time to pay for the twins' candy.

"You gave us a great fright," he said to Freddie and Flossie as they left the shop together. "You shouldn't have gone outside the gate."

The small twins apologized and offered the guide some of their candy. Nan and the headmistress were relieved to see the small Bobbseys again and glad that it had not been necessary to notify the police. The children thanked her for a very pleasant morning, and Nan said she was sorry it had ended with such a scare. The kindly headmistress smiled, remarking she knew that it was hard for a child in any country to resist a candy shop.

When the twins reached the hotel, Mr. and Mrs. Bobbsey were waiting for them. That afternoon their father took them to a moving-picture show. He did not tell them what it was going to be, and only Nan could read the Spanish sign outside the theater. As the story unfolded on the screen, Flossie became so excited she called out loudly in the dark, quiet theater:

"Duendes! Oh, Daddy, are they real little men or just make-believe people?"

Mr. Bobbsey whispered that it was not polite to talk in the theater. He added, "Maybe you will find out if you watch closely."

The first part of the story was based on an old Mexican legend. A mother, father, and their little boy lived in a house which was not kept very clean. The mother never had meals ready on time. Her small son, whose clothes were ragged, was very sad. One day, while he was in the woods, he met some duendes and told them his troubles.

The little elves decided to help him. They came to his house, but made themselves invisible. The mother could not see them, but she found herself working very hard, cleaning, cooking, and sewing. Actually, the little men whom she could not see were helping her. She found she did not mind doing the work at all, and when she saw how happy her family was, in a clean house, with a good dinner on the stove, she decided to do everything promptly from that time on.

The duendes went from place to place. Sometimes

they were very mischievous, but usually they did good deeds. The next part of the picture showed them among the cacao trees. Here they hid themselves, up in the tall, leafy branches. On the ground were two peons having an argument. The workmen would have got into a fight, but all of a sudden they began to be showered with cacao beans. They were so surprised that they stopped arguing and got to work. Up among the leaves the duendes laughed to themselves.

The last scene in the picture showed the little men going to a tumble-down hut. In it were a boy and a girl who had no parents and very little to eat or to wear. One of the duendes asked them if they would like to fly to the forest with them and live there.

"Oh, yes," the children cried.

From a little bag one man took out two pairs of wings and fastened them to the children's shoulders. Then, suddenly, wings stood up on the backs of all the duendes. A moment later they and the boy and girl were flying through the air.

"Oh, I guess they weren't real little men after all," Flossie said aloud.

It was all right for her to talk now, because the lights had gone on in the theater and the show was over. Freddie was quiet for some time, but finally he told his father he wished somebody would pin wings on him, so he could go to the forest also.

Mr. Bobbsey laughed. "Our wings will have to be airplane wings. But just keep on wishing real hard, Freddie. Maybe you'll get to the forest yet!"

All the twins wondered if their father's remark was a hint that they were going to take a trip to a Mexican forest. They knew he planned to look at some lumber, and hoped he would take them along. He did not say any more about it, but remarked that the next day Manuel was going to show them the pyramids.

Early the next morning the pleasant young man came to the hotel in his car, and the Bobbsey family set off. Manuel said that since they had plenty of time, he would take them first to a doll market. They drove for several miles, and then went up a steep hill.

The trees along the way were tall, and cast long shadows across the road as the bright sunlight slanted down between them. Soon they came to a little village with an old, yellow stone church and one store. In front of the store was a roof which extended across the whole sidewalk.

There were only a few houses in the town, but there were hundreds and hundreds of dolls. Under the shed and all along the shady sidewalk were tables filled with the toys. Wires were strung along here and there, and from these all sorts of dolls dangled. Some were carved of wood, others were made of straw, and a few were woven from grass. The best dolls were made of clay and painted. Some of them were very beautiful.

Flossie decided at once that she did not like the grotesque ones; men dolls with funny faces. She loved the baby dolls, and her mother told her she might pick out one to buy.

Ordinarily, Bert and Freddie were not interested in dolls, but when Bert spied a bullfighter and Freddie a Mexican fireman, they wanted to buy them. This left only Nan without a purchase. Her parents wondered if she were not interested, but Nan simply could not make up her mind which doll to choose.

"I'd like a funny one, and I'd like a serious one," she said. "But I guess I'll pick this Indian woman and her burro. She reminds me of that woman who put the live chickens in the car!"

Manuel urged the Bobbseys to leave, as they still had an hour's drive to the pyramids. Long before they reached the ancient pyramids, they could see the tall masses of stone. From a distance they looked pointed, and the twins were amazed to learn from Manuel that actually they were flat on top, and that there were steps leading up to the summit.

"Oh, I want to climb to the very top of the tallest one!" Freddie announced.

Manuel said there was no law against his doing this, but that it was a long way up for anyone with short legs.

"There is nothing at the pyramids now but ruins,"

the guide told them. "Once upon a time it was a good-sized city, but during a war, long ago, many of the buildings were destroyed, and since then the wind and dirt have swept over them. For several years our government has been carrying on digging operations, but it will take a long time to uncover the whole city."

"Will we be able to see how the people used to live?" Nan asked him.

The young man smiled. He said they would have to do a little guessing about this. Some strange writings had been found carved on stone, telling about the customs, but it was hard work figuring out what the symbols meant. Students at the university were busy working on this, and little by little they were gathering the story about how those ancient people lived.

"But I can show you a theater," Manuel said, and this was the first place they saw.

The theater was underground, and was very different from any the children had ever seen or heard about. The stage was a large, square platform set in the center. It was lower than the seats, which rose up like bleachers on all sides. Everything was made of a cementlike material, and colored a lovely soft shade of pink.

The twins hurried down the steps and climbed up to the stage. Freddie and Flossie did part of their elf act. Bert called out loudly, and waited to hear his echo. To his amazement there was no echo. He asked his mother, who was standing at the top of the stone bleachers, to listen to him while he spoke very softly.

"Can you hear me?" he asked in a voice only a little above a whisper.

"Yes, dear, I can," Mrs. Bobbsey replied, and again Bert was amazed. The ancient people certainly understood how to build their theaters in such a way that the actors' voices could be heard easily.

Manuel next showed the visitors part of an apartment house. The twins were astounded to learn that the ancient people had running water in their homes, and that it was carried to the city through a long aqueduct.

"It is thought that once there was a beautiful lagoon in the center of the city," Manuel told them, pointing to a long, grassy section. "I wonder if they had swans on the water," he said dreamily.

All the Bobbseys had a great deal of imagination. As they stood looking at the ruins, they had no trouble imagining how the place probably had looked long ago. Gazing up the long, narrow stretch they could see in their mind's eye the lovely body of water with flowers growing here and there in it. On the left and right were low, colored cement dwellings, and at the far end was a pyramid. Other pyramids were in the distance.

Manuel drove the visitors around to see the pyramids. Mrs. Bobbsey went to the top of one of the
small ones and down the other side to see some
marvelous stone carvings of animal heads and ser-
pents. But she decided that this was all the climbing
she was going to do.

Mr. Bobbsey, Manuel, and the twins set off for
the highest pyramid. Eagerly they started up the
slightly crumbled steps. It soon became evident that
the trip to the top was going to be too much for
Freddie and Flossie, so Nan offered to go back with
them and wait at the foot.

Up and up went the others. Bert reached the platform at the top long ahead of his father and Manuel.
He waved to his sisters and brother below, and then
started to walk across to the other side.

At this moment the wind began to blow. It blew
harder and harder, and the dust swirled all around.

"Oh," cried Flossie, "I can't stand still!"

She and Freddie were being forced into a run by
the strong wind. Nan was having a hard time standing up herself. But what was worse, she knew her
twin up on top of the pyramid was slowly being
pushed off. She could see Bert struggling to move
back from the edge.

Suddenly he disappeared!

CHAPTER XXIII

A NARROW ESCAPE

WITHIN two minutes the air around the pyramids was so filled with dust that no one could see where anyone else was. Flossie and Freddie, no longer able to stand up, were rolling along the ground.

Nan had been forced to lie flat to keep from being blown over. As she lay face down, her arms shielding her head, she worried about Bert. Had he been blown from the top of the pyramid? The thought made her shudder.

Mr. Bobbsey and Manuel were unable to stand up either. They had tried to climb to the top and help Bert, but the wind had forced them back. Now they were crawling on hands and knees around the pyramid to see if they could find Bert.

Poor Bert! The first gust of the sudden cyclone had thrown him down. He had tried hard to stay on the platform, but as the wind grew stronger, it rolled him over and over to the edge. For a moment he had clung to the top step, then had been forced off to the one below.

He got up, but the wind knocked him over again, and he slipped to the next lower step. Bert tried to lie flat, but he could not do this either. The cyclone whipped at him, shoving him down and down. Finally he reached the ground, his clothes torn, and the skin rubbed off all his knuckles.

As suddenly as it had come up, the wind stopped blowing. Bert, exhausted, closed his eyes. The next thing he knew, he heard voices and saw his mother standing over him.

"Are you all right, dear?" she was saying anxiously.

For a full second Bert was not sure whether or not he *was* all right. He was glad just to lie on the ground and say nothing. At first, he could not remember what had happened to him. Then, as he saw the pyramid that loomed above him, he remembered how the wind had blown him off the platform and caused him to slide all the way to the ground. He closed his eyes as if to shut out the frightening memory of it.

Then suddenly he felt better. He sat up and smiled at his mother.

"Sure. I'm all right," he said. Slowly he got to his feet.

By this time Mr. Bobbsey and Manuel had

reached the bottom of the pyramid. Finding that Bert had escaped injury, they hurried around to the far side of the pyramid, concerned over what might have happened to Nan and the small twins.

At first they could not see them anywhere, but finally Manuel spotted them. Hurrying to the children the men asked if they were all right.

"Just awful dusty," Flossie replied.

All of them were covered with dust, and the clothes of everyone except Mrs. Bobbsey had been ripped and snagged. Bert's coat and trousers were a sight.

"We'll be a strange-looking lot of people to the folks at the hotel," smiled Mrs. Bobbsey. "Manuel, is there any place where we could get fixed up a little before we return to the city?"

The young man said he could arrange it. As Nan looked around the vast expanse of ruins and grass, she wondered how he was going to do this. But Manuel seemed to be able to accomplish anything.

He led them to the parked car which fortunately had been out of the path of the wind. It was not harmed at all. The travelers climbed in and Manuel drove for half an hour. Then he came to a village, drew up in front of a house, and asked his passengers to wait outside a few minutes. He disappeared into the house but returned almost at once with a very pretty woman. Unlike most of the people in Mexico she had blue eyes and blonde hair. She greeted the Bobbseys in Spanish.

"This is my aunt," said Manuel. "She doesn't speak English, but she is delighted to meet you and will be very glad to help you out, if you will come inside. Her servants will clean your clothes."

Mrs. Bobbsey thanked them for their kindness, and the family followed her into the house. She and the girls were escorted to an attractive bedroom with gaily painted furniture. Mr. Bobbsey and the boys were taken to another bedroom. Their outer clothes were carried downstairs.

After the guests had washed and were waiting for their clothes, they were served cups of delicious chocolate and dainty pastries. As Mr. Bobbsey sipped his drink, he asked Manuel about the beautiful, dark-brown furniture in the room. He had never seen any wood like it, though he had been in the lumber business many years.

"I'm sorry, Señor. I don't remember the name of the wood," the guide answered. "My uncle bought it in the south of our country. It is rare and very few people have it."

Mr. Bobbsey decided to have a set of furniture like it made for the Bobbsey home, to surprise his family, if he could find the wood.

Presently there was a knock on the door and a

bright-eyed Indian boy came in with the clothes of
Mr. Bobbsey, Freddie, and Manuel. In halting English the Indian apologized that Bert's clothes were
in too bad a state to be mended. In their place he was
offering a new suit of his own which he had never
worn. The others were amazed as he held it up. It
might have come from a shop in Lakeport!

Mr. Bobbsey was sure that the suit must mean a
great deal to the Indian boy. Probably he had
saved his money for a long time to buy it. Offering
it to a total stranger was certainly a very fine gesture
on his part.

"Golly, that's swell," said Bert, then looked at his
father and added, "we'll pay for it, won't we?"

"Of course," Mr. Bobbsey replied.

"Oh, no," said the Indian. "You have bad luck at
pyramid. I make up and bring you good luck."

Manuel advised the Bobbseys to accept the offer.
Since Manuel understood the customs of the country
better than they, the twins' father thanked the Indian boy and took the suit from him.

When the family got together once more, Mrs.
Bobbsey and the girls stared at Bert. Manuel certainly was a magician. He had even found a new
suit for Bert!

It was not until they all were in the car and
driving away that Manuel explained about Mexi-

cans always being glad to help people in trouble. They did not want to be paid for their kindness, but they did like to hear from the people again.

"Would your nice aunt accept a little gift from us?" asked Mrs. Bobbsey.

"Yes," the guide replied and added with a grin, "and the Indian boy will be very glad to receive a new suit!"

Early the next morning Mrs. Bobbsey and Bert went shopping near the hotel. A suit very much like the new one Bert had on was sent to the Indian boy. Manuel's aunt would receive the lovely blouse they purchased.

Back at the hotel Mr. Bobbsey, Nan, and the younger twins were starting to pack. The twins' father had received word he would have to shorten his trip to Mexico. He had told his family that if they wanted to visit the Castillios before returning to Lakeport they would have to leave Mexico City at once. He had reserved seats on a plane and they would go directly after luncheon.

By the time Mrs. Bobbsey and Bert returned, the packing was finished and the bags taken to the airport by Manuel. It was not until he had gone that the twins' mother discovered a whole drawerful of her clothes and all the toilet articles had been left behind. There was nothing in which to pack them!

She rang for the chambermaid and Nan asked for a box, but the young woman shook her head.

"I guess there's only one thing to do," said Mrs. Bobbsey. "Nan, ask her where we can buy a suitcase."

Nan translated the request to the chambermaid, and the young woman's eyes sparkled.

"I will buy one for you at my cousin's shop," she assented in Spanish, and disappeared from the room.

Ten minutes later she reappeared carrying a very attractive bamboo, leather-trimmed suitcase. The young woman named a price for it which Mrs. Bobbsey thought was very reasonable, so she bought it at once.

"This is something I've always wanted," the twins' mother remarked. "It was lucky for me that you and Daddy forgot to pack some of my clothes!"

At two o'clock Manuel came to drive the Bobbseys to the airport. Mr. Bobbsey paid him for his kind services during their stay in Mexico City. Then he handed him a little envelope, saying it was a gift from the family in appreciation of all the things he had done for them.

Manuel peeped into the envelope and gasped. It contained several tickets to various games they knew he would like to see; *jai alai,* a bullfight, a horse race, and a baseball game.

"Caramba!" exclaimed Manuel, delighted.

Flossie and Freddie had heard this word several times since they had been in Mexico, but each time they had forgotten to find out what it meant. Now they asked Manuel.

"I guess in your country you would say 'gosh,' " he laughed. "Well, good-bye," he added, as the passengers were called to the plane. *"Hasta la vista!* Good-bye!"

The Bobbseys hurried aboard and took their seats. A few minutes later they were in the air on their way to the Castillios' hacienda.

"Caramba!" exclaimed Freddie suddenly.

CHAPTER XXIV

THE CHOCOLATE TREES

FREDDIE Bobbsey had spoken loudly, but had not pronounced the Spanish word very well. Everyone in the place laughed. At first Freddie's mother thought he had said it because he had forgotten something he meant to bring. But she found out he was merely happy, and used this new word because he liked it.

"Caramba!" he said over and over, until his father stopped him.

During the rest of the journey Freddie was quiet. Part of the time he looked at a picture book, and the rest of the time he looked out the window.

After a while the twins noticed that the scenery below them had changed. They were now flying over territory they were sure must be a jungle. Half an hour later, the pilot circled and then started down. The Bobbseys were about to land near the Castillios' hacienda.

"There's Mateo!" Bert cried out, as the plane rolled to a stop.

"And I see Marina!" exclaimed Flossie.

When the visitors got out, they realized it was very warm, far warmer than it had been in Mexico City. The Castillio children wore thin clothes and large straw hats. The Lakeport children decided to change their clothes as soon as possible.

Pedro was there also, and said that Mrs. Castillio was sorry not to have been able to come to welcome them. She could not stand the heat.

"My father had to see about his cacao trees to-day," Mateo said. "That is why he did not come. But he will be home by the time we get there."

"Is it far to your house?" Flossie asked, not seeing any buildings.

Pedro told them it would take half an hour to drive to the house. They all got into the large car, though even then it was a tight squeeze. The road was not very good, and they had to go slowly, but it was beautiful along the way. There were eucalyptus trees a hundred feet tall, and back of these were forests of many varieties of wood. Nan asked if any of them were cacao trees, but was told these forests were a mixture of mahogany and rosewood.

"In one place on our hacienda we grow chewing gum trees." Mateo smiled. "They are called chicle."

Flossie and Freddie wanted to see these trees, but Pedro said they were miles away from the house.

The twins could hardly believe a hacienda could be that big!

As they rode along, they saw pineapples growing in their huge, cactuslike plants, then banana trees. The twins were amazed to see the bunches of bananas standing upright.

"I guess they always sell them upside down in stores," Flossie remarked. "Why do they grow with their points up in the air?"

Pedro grinned. "Maybe it's so the monkeys can eat them easily," he teased.

Sometime later the Bobbseys heard a bell tolling. It could be heard a long distance, and Pedro explained that it called the workers home in the evening.

Flossie giggled. "It's calling us, too."

"Oh, there's the house!" Nan said, as she recognized it from the pictures the Castillios had shown them.

There was the wall with the beautiful flowers growing on it. And towering above everything was the mansion. Pedro stopped the car at a huge wooden gate, which was opened by a smiling boy, and then drove through.

The photographs of the Castillios' home had not shown how lovely the place really was. It was far more beautiful than any other the twins had ever seen.

Indeed, it was like fairyland. Bright-colored birds flitted from tree to tree, chirping happily. A cunning little monkey looked down from a branch and chattered saucily at them.

"He is a pet," said Marina. "We will play with him tomorrow."

There were pools of water, in which exquisitely colored goldfish were swimming. Flowers grew everywhere.

When the Bobbseys arrived at the front door, Anita was waiting there. Two boys appeared to take the bags. Pedro and Anita escorted the visitors into the mansion. How beautiful it was inside! And how cool! It was a relief to get away from the heat.

Mrs. Castillio came at once to greet them and make her friends welcome. They were taken to a wing of the house on the second floor, where there were a sitting room and three bedrooms for them. Mrs. Castillio remarked that no doubt the Bobbseys would like to bathe before dinner.

"This is the time of day when we Mexicans begin to play," she smiled. "If the children would like to go swimming, Mateo and Marina will take them."

The Bobbsey twins could think of nothing they would like to do better. It did not take them long to put on the bathing suits they had brought. Mateo and Marina led them to one of the walled gardens; in fact, it was the one where the old stone frog squirted water from its mouth. In a corner of this garden was a good-sized swimming pool with a diving board at one end.

Mateo and Marina were expert swimmers. Bert and Nan could swim and dive very well too, but Freddie and Flossie were beginners. They were amazed that little Marina could swim so much better than they could. With her usual politeness Marina remarked:

"If you lived where it is warm all the time, you would swim a lot too. And when you swim a lot, you learn to swim very well."

The small Bobbsey twins found, during their first two days with the Castillios, that they had to change their habits somewhat. They got up later in the morning than they were accustomed to doing, and had breakfast in the garden. At two o'clock the children would be served a light meal and would then go to bed until five. From five to eight they would play, and at nine o'clock in the evening they would have dinner.

Dinner turned out to be a meal with so many courses the small twins could eat only half of what was served. After the second day the visitors learned Marina usually did not stay up so late. But, knowing that at home Flossie and Freddie ate with their parents, the Castillios thought that was what the Bobbseys would like. Everyone laughed, and after this Marina, Flossie, and Freddie had dinner at seven-thirty, and then went to bed soon afterward.

Bert and Nan thought it was fun to stay awake, and after the second day found they did not get sleepy until nearly midnight. Mrs. Bobbsey remarked that they were becoming completely spoiled.

"I guess I am," Nan said, as she kissed her mother good night on retiring. "It's so wonderful here I'm afraid I don't ever want to go home."

Mrs. Bobbsey told her they would have to leave in a few days, nevertheless; as soon as the twins' father had completed his business deal on the lumber. He had gone off on a trip with Mr. Castillio to see about it. When Flossie heard they were to leave soon, she grew a bit worried.

"I haven't found any little men for that nice Captain Night," she told her mother. "Aren't we going to the forest where they live?"

Mrs. Bobbsey smiled. "There are legends about dwarfs who lived here in Mexico long, long ago," she said. "And some people, even today, believe that the dwarfs' great—many times great—grandchildren live hidden among the trees. But you mustn't be disappointed, Flossie, if you can't find them," she finished, patting her small daughter on the shoulder.

"But Captain Night's little men came from Mexico," Flossie pointed out.

"Well, we'll just have to think of those little men

as duendes whom we can't see," Mrs. Bobbsey concluded. "Now, suppose you find the other children
and tell them that tomorrow we'll take a trip to see
how chocolate is made."

That evening Mr. Bobbsey and Mr. Castillio returned. They had found just the right trees for Mr.
Bobbsey to buy, and he was glad he had made the
trip to Mexico. He had even bought some of the
beautiful, rare wood to have furniture made for his
family.

Early the next morning two cars of travelers set
out for the chocolate factory, with Pedro in charge.
They drove for a few miles until they came to a
village. In a stream of water on the outskirts Indian
women were washing their clothes. Their older children played around, while the babies lay asleep on
blankets on the ground. Near by were some of the
thatch-roofed cottages which the Bobbseys had seen
in the Castillios' photograph album.

"They don't look much like the hut I made at
home out of hay," Freddie remarked. "The one that
somebody burned up."

"I wonder if Charlie's found out yet who did it,"
mused Bert.

In the center of the Mexican town were pink, blue,
and yellow-colored buildings. Many natives were
coming and going. It seemed to the Bobbsey twins
as if everyone walking in the streets was carrying

something on his head; fruit, meat, flowers, furniture, or toys.

On the far side of town was the chocolate factory; only it was not a chocolate factory like the one Mr. Castillio had in Lakeport. Most of it was out of doors under a long roof.

The cars were parked, and Pedro took the Bobbsey family on a tour. First he showed them the purplish-colored pods from the cacao trees. They resembled warty pickles, and each one weighed about a pound. Inside them were flat, brown beans in a slimy, sweet syrup.

"They smell nice," Flossie remarked.

"Yes," Pedro replied. "But inside the beans the taste is very bitter."

He led the children to where thousands of the beans had been put in covered boxes to stay for a while and ferment. After this they would be dried.

"Then they are ready for the market," said Pedro. "But we do not send all of ours to market. We make cans of cocoa from some of them, and chocolate candy from others."

"Where's the candy factory?" Freddie asked at once.

Pedro told them it was too warm here to make much candy. Mr. Castillio's main factory was many miles away, where it was cooler. But Pedro did show the children where the cacao beans were crushed to a powder and the oil squeezed out of them, to get them ready for the candy making.

"Why do they take the oil out?" Nan inquired.

Pedro smiled. "It is really better for people to use cacao oil outside of their bodies than inside," he said. "The oil is rather hard to digest, but it is very lovely for the skin. But come now, we must hurry if we want to see the trees before it gets too hot."

The Bobbseys found the Castillio children and they set off for the cacao forest. When they reached it, they saw many men at work. Each one held a long pole. Whenever one of them could not reach the pods with his hands, he would reach high overhead and knock the pods down from among the leaves with his pole.

Freddie and Flossie were interested in a two-wheeled cart, drawn by an ox, which stood near by. Freddie asked Pedro if they could go for a ride in the cart, and he nodded. He hopped aboard with them, and off they went.

The small Bobbsey twins had never ridden in an oxcart before. They thought it was lots of fun, though the cart bounced up and down so hard they could barely stay on the seat. After they had ridden for ten minutes along the only road from which the jungle underbrush had been cleared, Pedro decided to turn around. But in doing so, the cart tilted and the wheel on Pedro's side came off. The three passengers slid to the ground.

"Caramba!" yelled Pedro.

"Caramba!" echoed Freddie.

Then Pedro laughed. He said it would take a few minutes to put the wheel back on. The children might look around a bit, but they were not to go far away from him. The small twins had no intention of walking any distance away from Pedro. It would be dreadful to be lost in this cacao jungle!

Suddenly Flossie thought she saw something moving behind the thick bushes. She tiptoed a little closer to look. Then, hardly able to believe her eyes, she cried out:

"Duende!"

CHAPTER XXV

FLOSSIE'S DISCOVERY

IN HER excitement Flossie Bobbsey ran forward quickly.

"Duende! Duende!" she kept calling.

The little person behind the bushes stood still and peered at her. Flossie had a hard time pushing aside the thick stems of the bush to get around to the back. Then she stood still and stared. Was she dreaming?

Before her stood not one, but two little men no taller than herself. They did not have on green suits or pointed caps; in fact, all they wore were light brown pants nearly the color of their skin.

The dwarfs grinned at Flossie. When she could find her voice, she asked them if they were duendes. They looked at each other, then at her, but did not say a word.

"Oh, I guess they don't understand me," said Flossie. "What'll I do?"

The little girl already was trying to figure out how

she could take these tiny men with her. Now she could keep her promise to Captain Friday Night! Flossie held out her hands toward them. They seemed to know it was a gesture of friendship, and willingly followed her, as she made her way back to Pedro and Freddie.

"Caramba!" exclaimed Pedro.

For once Freddie was speechless, but presently he asked his twin where she had found the little men. In the meantime, Pedro spoke to the dwarfs in Spanish, but they shook their heads. Next he tried an Indian language used by some of the people who lived in the near-by village. Again the little men shook their heads.

Pedro now pointed to the oxcart. He had fixed the wheel and was ready to return. The little men did not seem to know what he meant, so Pedro lifted Freddie up onto the seat. Then he took hold of one of the dwarfs and started to put him into the cart. At this the little man let out a screech and backed away.

Just at that moment a tall Indian came up the road. Mr. Bobbsey had become worried about his children, and had asked the man to go and look for them.

When the Indian saw the two little men, he, too, stared. He spoke to them in a language not familiar to Pedro, but the two little men understood it. Bobbing their heads excitedly, they answered him in their squeaky voices.

Flossie became very excited. "Oh, tell them!" she cried out, "that we want them to go with us."

The Indian did not understand her, but Pedro interpreted for her. What a strange conversation went on—in three different languages! At last the dwarfs understood that a man in a faraway country, with a big boat, wanted them to come and live on it.

The Bobbseys in turn learned that the little men belonged to a tribe of people who live deep in the jungle, and that practically no one knows about them. They gave directions, however, about where to find them, and suggested that the man with the big boat come down there to see them.

Flossie was disappointed that she could not take the dwarfs right along with her. But Pedro said it would be better if Captain Friday Night attended to that himself. As they jogged back in the oxcart, Flossie looked up at Pedro and said:

"Those men were real, live men, weren't they?"

"Of course," Pedro replied. "Why do you ask?"

"Then they're not duendes?" she said.

Pedro smiled. "More likely they are descendants of dwarfs who lived here long, long ago, and they're real. Some people claim duendes are real, too, but I am sure it is only in dreams that a person can see a duende or any other kind of fairy."

Freddie and Flossie thought about this all the way back to the hacienda. During the next two days they talked a great deal between themselves, trying to figure out how much of what they had seen and heard in Mexico had been real, and how much of it they might have dreamed. The twins had seen so many different kinds of homes and people, and had heard so many languages spoken, it seemed as if they must have read some of it in fairy tales.

Bert was more practical about the whole thing. Upon hearing about the little men of the forest, he immediately wrote a letter to Captain Friday Night at the address the owner of the traveling amusement park had given him.

There was only one thing during the whole vacation in Mexico that might have spoiled the twins' fun. This had nothing whatever to do with the interesting Land of Sunshine. It was a letter Bert received from Charlie Mason the day before they were to leave. The Lakeport boy said he had tracked down the person who had burned up Freddie's hut. He was none other than the mean Danny Rugg!

"But you won't have to worry about fighting him," Charlie wrote. "Danny got the scare of his life. The police got after him and gave him a talking-to for starting the fire."

Bert and the others put the matter out of their minds, and enjoyed their last day at the hacienda with their Mexican friends. Then they packed their belongings, including the many little gifts they were going to take home. Mr. Bobbsey surprised his sons by giving them a reed chair for their bedroom. It would be shipped to Lakeport. The next morning they bade the Castillios good-bye and boarded the plane that was to start them on their journey back to the United States.

As the twins talked over the many adventures they had had in Mexico, they wondered if any trip the family might take in the future could possibly be so wonderful. They had a surprise in store for them, as one may find out in THE BOBBSEY TWINS' TOY SHOP.

"What did you like best of all in Mexico?" Mrs. Bobbsey asked her children, when, at last, they were only a few miles away from Lakeport.

Bert declared that while he did not like it at the time, he was glad to have had his adventure at the pyramid. "I'll bet not many boys have been blown off a pyramid," he laughed. "It sure was scary."

Nan said she enjoyed the days at the beautiful Castillio hacienda, and wished she might have brought the pet monkey back with her. Freddie was sorry he had not seen a fire in Mexico, but at least he had a fireman doll from that country. And it was fun to have fallen in the water at the floating gardens.

Flossie was the last one to answer her mother's question. Finally she said:

"I loved everything in Mexico. But most of all, now, I love the silver duende the man at the factory gave me. I'll always have it to look at to remind me of Mexico."